# Imperfect Stranger

By

Doris Reidy

ISBN-10: 1983999318
ISBN-13: 978-1983999314

# Also by Doris Reidy

*Mrs. Entwhistle*
*Every Last Stitch*
*Five for the Money*

# Dedication

I am blessed with an incredible family and wonderful friends. This book is for them.

# Chapter One

It happened right in front of me. Visibility on the narrow mountain road was almost zero in the rain and fog. I heard the crash before I saw it, pulled over and got out of my car.

It's still there when I close my eyes. The car hanging at a crazy angle over the sharp embankment; the guardrail a twisted pretzel, all that kept the car from falling; the dead deer sprawled on the road. I stood there for what seemed an eon. What do I do? Will my touch tip the car out of balance and make it plunge over the cliff? Should I call for help, wait for reinforcements? Surely someone else heard the crash or saw the crazy headlights pointing to the sky. My paralysis was broken by a tentative little voice.

"Mama?"

I approached the car, careful not to brush against it, and looked through the rear side window. A small face looked back at me. In the front seat, the driver was curled into the deflated airbag, motionless. I could see it was a woman.

My mind bounced between options, none of which were good.

Carefully, I tried the front door, but it didn't budge. The driver's side window was gone. Reaching through it, I placed my hand on the woman's neck, feeling for a pulse the way I'd seen it done so many times on television. Apparently it's easier on T.V., because I felt nothing. I pulled away a hand smeared with blood. The baby whimpered again.

"Hang on," I said, my voice coming out in a croak. "Hang on, kid. I'll get you out."

Holding my breath, willing my hands to be steady, I painstakingly tried the back door. It opened one creak at a time. I fumbled with the unfamiliar straps and latches of the baby's car seat. Just as I lifted the small body clear, the car lurched sickeningly and resettled.

The baby seemed okay. I sat her on the ground and went back to the woman. Awake now, she was making feeble attempts to climb out of the window. Our eyes met, hers pleading.

"Emmy?" she said.

There was a smell of gasoline, pungent and dangerous. All it needed was a spark. I was out of time. I grabbed the woman's arms and pulled hard. She screamed as the car pulled in the opposite direction, convulsed and disappeared almost soundlessly. We fell backwards to the ground, to safety, the woman and I. I eased her carefully onto the ground next to her baby, who stopped crying and sucked her thumb, holding a fistful of her mother's hair. The woman's forehead leaked blood that almost obscured her face, but her eyes held mine. I fumbled for my cell phone, dialed 911 and gave our location.

That's when I should have gotten in my car and driven on, but the woman's hand caught mine and held. I sat beside them and waited.

Sirens and blue lights announced the arrival of the ambulance and the sheriff. After paramedics screamed off with their

2

patients, the cop got out his little notebook and asked my name. My mouth opened to lie. But what I said, sweating, my heart galloping, was the truth: "John Carver."

If he runs it, he runs it. No point in trying to hide. Not now.

~*~

The light hurt my eyes. I tried to lift my arm to shield them, but my arm didn't seem to be working, so I turned my head. Only my neck didn't seem to be working, either.

"Emmy?" I said, or maybe I only thought it.

"Hold still, don't move."

I could see nothing – what was wrong with my eyes? I smelled disinfectant. I felt the stiffness of my body. I heard shoes squeaking on the floor, murmurs, snatches of talk. It didn't make sense, but all that mattered was...

"Emmy!" I said again, stronger, and this time the voice came close to my ear.

"You've been in a bad accident, Bree. Now, don't you worry, honey, your little girl is just fine. That car seat really did its job tonight."

"Where's she?" I slurred.

"Your mom came and got her. Emmy was so glad to see her grandma. You never saw such a big smile."

If Emmy was smiling, then all was well. I slept.

~*~

I'd discovered that not only were there no motels in Grand Butte, everything closed down at night. Parked in front of a dark restaurant, I fished the emergency blanket out of the trunk, curled up on the back seat and slept. It wasn't the first time I'd ever slept in my car. The instinct to escape was strong, but the cop's parting words last night had been,

"Appreciate it if you'd stick around; I've got a few more questions." Something in his eyes told me I'd better do as he said.

I woke stiff, cold and hungry. My fingers still had blood around the nail beds and I longed for a steaming shower and a hot cup of coffee, but it looked like the only doable thing was the coffee. The restaurant's lights went on and soon I was sitting at the counter. I was deep into my third cup when the sheriff entered and approached me. What had he said his name was? I caught a look at his badge: Dawson.

"Morning, Mr. Carver," he said, hitching one leg over a stool. The waitress came over right away with the coffee pot. "Good morning, Patsy," he added.

"Mornin', Daw," she replied, pouring him a cup without being asked, pushing the cream and sugar toward him. "Awful about the wreck last night. Are Bree and Emmy going to be okay?"

"I think so," Sheriff Dawson said. "Bree's in the hospital. She's got some broken bones and facial cuts, but Emmy went home with her grandma last night."

"Oh, that's good news about Emmy, anyway." She looked at me and asked, "Ready for a refill?"

"Just half a cup," I said. "I'll be climbing the walls as it is."

"Patsy, Mr. Carver, here, was the first one on the scene of the accident last night. He pulled Emmy and Bree from the car just before it went over the side of Butte Mountain," Sheriff Dawson said.

Patsy beamed, reached under a glass dome and plucked out a huge sugared doughnut which she plopped down before me. "On the house," she said. "You're a hero."

I fought the urge to look over my shoulder for the real hero.

It couldn't possibly be me. These people were nice and all, but if they knew…Well, I wouldn't be sitting here eating a free doughnut, that's for sure. I turned my attention back to the sheriff.

"Mr. Carver, I thank you and the whole town thanks you for what you did."

"It was luck, mostly," I said. "Just happened to be on the spot. Anybody would have done what I did."

"That's not true. You kept your head. If you hadn't, Bree and her little girl might have gone over the cliff with the car. I'd like to review your statement, if you don't mind, just make sure I've got it all right. Then you can be on your way if you want. We don't want to keep you from anything important."

He looked at me expectantly, so I felt obliged to say, "That's okay, I'm not in any hurry." But I was. The combination of caffeine, sugar and a need to flee had me shaking. I put my hands in my lap so he wouldn't see.

"This is a small town," the sheriff said, as if I might not have noticed. "We all know each other here, and when somebody gets hurt, we're all concerned."

Looking at his open and innocent face, I knew he hadn't bothered to look me up. He continued.

"I've known Bree since she was a baby. She comes from a mighty fine family, good salt of the earth folks. My wife went to a shower for little Emmy."

I nodded, unsure what to say.

"We're grateful. I know I speak for Bree and her family, too. We're grateful that a perfect stranger risked his own life to save two of our own."

"Uh, thank you, Sheriff Dawson."

"You call me Daw," he said. "Everybody does."

He turned to Patsy and said, "Here, that's mine, honey," and she handed him my bill. I nodded my thanks, reminding myself that it was just a cup of coffee. I didn't owe him anything.

"How long..." I began. There didn't seem to be a gracious way to ask how long I'd have to stay in the company of these nice people. But he knew what I was going to say.

"Not too much longer, although we'd be glad to keep you around as long as you'd like to stay," he said. "I'm going over to my office and complete the paperwork right now, and then I'll ask you to sign a witness statement. It's probably not even important, but I'm just trying to make sure every loose thread is tied up before Bree files an insurance claim for her car. Those insurance companies, they don't like to pay out, do they?"

We shook our heads over the wicked ways of insurers.

"Meanwhile, I apologize for not thinking you'd have to sleep in your car last night after I asked you to stick around. Grand Butte doesn't have a motel, but I should have taken you home with me," he went on. "Let me do that now. I bet a nice, hot shower would be welcome."

"Oh, no, really, thanks, I couldn't impose on you like that," I said, although nothing could have sounded better.

"No imposition whatsoever," he said, slapping me on the back, man to man." You get cleaned up while my wife cooks you a good breakfast. Not that Patsy, here, wouldn't feed you well."

The sheriff winked and Patsy laughed. My mind raced, trying to figure out a plausible escape. Landing in the home of local law enforcement did not strike me as a good idea. But somehow, I found myself hustled out the door, the sheriff's arm around my shoulder, heading toward my car.

"Uh oh, look at that," the sheriff said, pointing. The car tilted at an angle, one side definitely higher than the other. The cause was immediately apparent: two flat tires on the left side. I squatted down to inspect the damage.

"Looks like I picked up some metal scraps," I said. "This one is pretty well shredded. Back one looks about the same."

"You picked 'em up at the scene of Bree's wreck, I guess," Daw said. "There was stuff all over the highway. No good deed goes unpunished, right? Well, we'll get you fixed up."

I'd bought the car at the first used car lot I'd come to after...afterward. I just needed wheels, a way to get out of Dodge. The car was old, but it ran. I'd had enough cash left for gas and fast food. That was all I needed.

Now, some itchy premonition made me unlock the driver's side door and slip behind the wheel. I put my key in the ignition and turned it. I heard a click. Tried again. Click.

Daw shook his head. "Looks like you've got more problems than a couple of flats," he said. "I'll have Doug take a look at it."

We stopped by the town's only garage on the way to Daw's house and I met Doug. He said he'd run over to the restaurant and tow my car to the shop. He shook his head when I described the click.

"Sounds like the starter. We'll probably have to order it. We don't keep 'em in stock for a car that old," he said.

"How long will that take?" I asked.

"Oh, 'bout a week, I guess. I order parts off the Internet. Depends on where they're coming from as to how fast they'll get here."

A week! This day was not shaping up to be much better than the previous one. Daw took the news in stride. "Good thing you've got a place to stay," was all he said.

"No, it's too much of an imposition," I protested again. "Your wife won't want to be bothered with a guest for a week."

"Janie? Why, there's nothing she likes better than having company. Somebody to cook for, now that the kids are gone."

I couldn't think of any other objections without sounding like an ungrateful jerk, so I shut up, climbed into the squad car and went home with the sheriff.

~*~

After I felt a little better and my headache subsided to a dull pain I could almost ignore, I did a lot of thinking in the hospital. A forced time-out like that allows one's mind to churn up all kinds of stuff from the past. My name, for instance. I wonder how different my life might have been if I'd stayed Brenna Kathleen Carrolton, instead of becoming Bree. Mom named me Brenna after her mother and Kathleen after herself. I thought it was a beautiful name, and felt proud to be another bead on the family chain. My grandmother died when I was too little to remember her, and I guess that's when I became Bree. When I went to first grade, I begged Mom to call me Brenna like my teacher did, but she said it made her too sad. After a while, even the teachers called me Bree.

I wondered if Brenna would have been a different person. Someone with common sense and good judgment. Someone settled and patient and sweet.

As I lay there on the uncomfortable hospital bed, I reviewed my whole life. I grew up in Grand Butte (yes, of course, every generation of kids called it Grand Butt), but not until I was an adult would I fully appreciate our little town. It was just a wide spot in the road, snuggled into the mountains, cut off from the wider world. I imagined it was like Brigadoon, the magical Scottish village that appeared only once every hundred years. Life was simple and easy in Brigadoon – and in Grand Butte. Everybody knew everybody, and their Uncle

Joe's cat. All parents supervised all children, and if we misbehaved, we could count on at least three phone calls making it home before we did. A secure existence, but also claustrophobic. At least, my teenage self found it so.

I was a wild child, always testing boundaries, stretching the patience of my mom and dad like taffy. I didn't want to hold Mom's hand crossing the street. I refused to come in when Dad called my name into the gathering dusk, not if there were still other kids outside, a game to be finished or a firefly to be captured. Sitting quietly at my desk in school was a torment. My body would twitch with the effort, and inevitably, I'd get up and look out the window, sharpen my pencils down to the erasers, make a dozen trips to the water fountain. Teachers complained: "Bree lacks self-control. Bree needs to work on her listening skills." Nowadays, I might have been given a more clinical label, like oppositional defiant disorder, and medicated. Then, I was sighed over, probably prayed over, but basically respected as a child who was having trouble finding her way.

Of course, the brunt of my bad behavior fell on my poor parents. They scolded and reasoned, tried time out, took away privileges. Sometimes, when pushed beyond exasperation, they spanked. I simply ignored them, intent on whatever interested me at that moment.

"She'll grow out of it," they repeated to each other like a mantra. And I did grow out of some of it, but the spark of rebellion remained. When I reached adolescence, hormones fanned that spark into a flame. I developed a taste for bad boys.

There weren't many in Grande Butte, but one was all I needed. His name was Billy Ketchum, but he insisted on being called Billy Idol from fifth grade on. Billy's parents lived on what passed for the wrong side of the tracks. Their house was small, in need of paint among other things, and filled with children and dogs. I liked to go there because of the dogs, even though Mom said, "No, you definitely may not." Billy and I played together in his littered yard, running with the pack. Then there came a hiatus in our friendship, along about middle school, when I tried, I really tried, to conform. It seemed important then to be like everybody else, even if it meant sanding down all my rough edges.

It didn't work. When I laid eyes on Billy Idol on the first day of high school, all my rough edges returned intact. Somehow over the summer, Billy'd turned into a bona fide idol. Tall, dark, with a face like Michelangelo's David, he was totally unconcerned about being liked and following the rules.

If he noticed me, he didn't let on. His eyes flickered for just a second when they met mine. After that, he ignored me, insuring that he'd burn like a flame in my imagination. What could have been more attractive to a girl who'd been trying, against the grain, to be good? What other outcome could there have been than that I chased him unashamedly?

And oh, yeah, I caught him. By sophomore year, we were a couple. My parents wrung their hands and talked late into the night while they waited for their fifteen-year-old daughter to come home, flushed, disheveled, once with my blouse inside-out. Mom had "the talk" with me; Dad threatened to have Billy arrested for statutory rape. Didn't matter. We were just biding our time, Billy and me. We had plans to blow this two-bit town the minute we graduated. New York City, here we'd come. We had no idea what we'd do when we got there, just some vague plans to support ourselves by waiting tables until we hit the big time, whatever that was.

Graduation day we refused to walk in procession with our classmates. Instead we went skinny-dipping at a lake high up the mountain. Our bodies looked like silver fish as we cut through the water, always ending up in each other's arms.

Billy seemed different that day, withdrawn one minute, clutching me the next.

"What's wrong?" I kept asking.

"Nothing, just glad to be done with that damn school," he answered.

But he wasn't himself. I thought, okay, everyone's entitled to a funny mood now and then, right? I decided my news could wait.

The next day, when Billy didn't call or blow the horn of his old car at the curb, I finally went to his house. It was locked up, the dogs milling around in their outdoor pen. Strange, because his house had never been locked in my memory. Somebody was always home. I sat on the porch swing until Billy's dad's car swung into the driveway.

"Mr. Ketchum, where's Billy?" I asked as soon as he had one leg out of the car. Mrs. Ketchum hurried past me, eyes down, unlocked the door as fast as she could and disappeared inside. Mr. Ketchum was left to do the dirty work.

"Well, now, Billy's gone," he said, looking past me at something invisible.

"Gone? What do you mean? Gone where?"

"Why, into the Army," Mr. Ketchum said, as if it were the most obvious of truths.

"What? He didn't say anything to me about joining the Army," I said. "When did this come up? Why didn't he tell me?"

"Billy had a choice, you see," Mr. Ketchum said. "Daw said he could enlist, or he could go to jail."

"Go to jail? For what?"

"I guess he didn't tell you about that, either. He got caught boosting a car."

"But when? When would he have done that? We were together every night," I said. All I could seem to do was ask questions. I had a thick feeling in my head, like there was a wall between me and the answers.

"Sometimes after he took you home, Billy would meet up with the guys. They'd get to drinking pretty heavy, and things happened. Daw looked the other way as much as he thought he could, but the car, that was the last straw. Billy didn't have the heart to tell you himself."

I couldn't speak. In a town where everybody knew everything, how could I not have known this? Mr. Ketchum looked embarrassed and uncomfortable. He shuffled his feet. Then he said, "Well, I'd best be gettin' inside."

That was my signal to leave. Move along, folks. Nothing to see here. Mechanically, I stood and walked away, dragging it behind me - the news I'd come to tell Billy.

~*~

So there I was, in Daw and Janie's spare room. I guessed it used to be their daughter's digs, judging from the frilly white curtains and canopy bed. I was a large and uncouth interloper, but oh, did that shower feel good.

Janie was tiny, all smiles and home cooking, the perfect complement to Daw's laconic lawman style. She whipped up a spread of bacon, eggs, pancakes and fruit and had it waiting on the table when I went downstairs. They were genuinely welcoming, Janie and Daw, and I tried to hide my uneasiness.

Doug called from the garage and reported that my old crate now boasted two new tires, and in a week or so would have a new starter. Trouble was, I didn't have enough money to pay for them.

"Daw, I was wondering," I began. "Do you know of any odd jobs I might do while I'm waiting? I don't want to just sit around, I like to be busy."

"Well," Daw said, drawing it out as he thought, "there're a few widows who are always looking for help with things around the house. Probably wouldn't pay much, though. The old dears like to hang onto their money. Do you have any particular skills?"

"I've worked in healthcare," I said. "Just as an orderly, or aide, or whatever you'd call it."

"What about Charles Jacoby?" Janie asked. "He's home from rehab after breaking his hip. He's alone in that great big house. His housekeeper will keep him fed, but he needs more help than that."

"How long do you figure you'd stay?" Daw asked bluntly. "No point in starting something and then leaving in a couple days."

"I can't commit to anything long-term," I said. "I'm just passing through and if it hadn't been for the accident, I'd never have stopped in Grand Butte at all. But it looks like I'll be here for about a week. Would that be of any help to Mr. Jacoby?"

"It might be. All we can do is ask," Janie said, and that's what she did. "He'd like to meet you," she reported after holding a lengthy phone conversation with the gentleman in question. "He asked if we could come over after supper."

The Jacoby house was a huge, brick monolith perched on a low hill, looking down its nose at the winding driveway. Gravel crunched under the tires as Daw, Janie and I arrived at a studded wooden door set in a stone arch. I looked around for the moat. Daw didn't seem to notice the Gothic atmosphere, and Janie nonchalantly rapped on the door with the polished brass knocker. There was a longish pause, but finally the door opened to reveal a very old man hanging onto

13

a walker for all he was worth.

"Hello, my dear," he said, his face breaking into a million-wrinkle smile when he saw Janie. "Daw, good evening. And you must be the town's new hero," he said, pumping my hand with surprising strength. "Come in, come in, all of you."

After pleasantries were exchanged in the wide front hall, we trooped into what I could only think must be the drawing room. A round table sat squarely in the middle of a faded Oriental rug. It held a bowl of flowers, a tray for mail and a basket for miscellany like keys and a dog leash. Muffled barking came from another part of the house. A fire crackled in a large stone fireplace, surrounded by deep easy chairs, to which Mr. Jacoby motioned us.

"I heard how you rescued Bree and Emmy," Mr. Jacoby said, after we were seated. "Thank you, Mr. Carver, for saving two of our own. I've known Bree, of course, since she was born. She's my great-niece. And now I know her daughter, my great-great niece. I'm thankful they are still with us, thanks to your courage and quick action."

"Uh, sure, my pleasure," I said awkwardly. I didn't know how to respond to praise. I'd not had much practice.

"And now you're looking for something to do while you wait for your car repair," Mr. Jacoby went on. He was certainly well informed of my situation. "I broke my hip slipping in the shower," he went on, "and after the operation, I spent two months in a rehab facility. I was just released day before yesterday. It's wonderful to be back in my home, but I'm finding that I could use a little help getting back into the swing of things. I don't view my need as being long-term."

"I only expect to be here for a week," I said.

"A week might be about right. I have a housekeeper who cooks and cleans, and a man who keeps the grounds. They don't come every day, though, and they go home at night. What I need right now is help with showering and dressing in the morning, and getting ready for bed at night."

His old face flushed a faint pink. I saw that this proud man hated asking for help.

"Then it would be nice to have someone who could take me out a bit – drives, a little shopping, maybe a meal or a movie. Just to keep my sanity, you know," he said with one of his wrinkled smiles. "I would prefer that you live here so you'd be available when I need you." He named a sum of money that made my mouth water. "Would that be agreeable?"

"Now Charles, you're stealing away my houseguest," Janie scolded. "And bribing him at that! But I can see you need him, and it sounds like an ideal arrangement for the short term."

"Understand, I would never invite a stranger into my home were it not for Daw's approval. He's a superior judge of character," Mr. Jacoby said. He pinned me with his faded blue eyes and I felt like I'd just been strip-searched.

I had no response to that. If you only knew, was my thought. I hoped it didn't show on my face.

# Chapter Two

A couple of broken ribs, some superficial facial cuts, one deep gash in my forehead that had to be stitched, and some broken bones in my right foot. Not too bad an outcome, considering the severity of the crash. The broken ribs were the worst. Every deep breath sent a knife-like pain shooting through my chest. And yet, deep breaths were necessary to keep from getting pneumonia, the nurse said, handing me the hateful little tube to blow into. Tears streamed down my face, but I did it. I needed to get out of this hospital bed and back to Emmy. My folks had her, I knew she was okay, but she had to be wondering what happened to me.

Mom popped in several times a day, leaving Emmy home with Grandpa. I heard her heels tapping in the corridor before I saw her face peeking around the door.

"Hellooo," she always said, as if she was a neighbor stopping in for coffee. She'd settle herself in the only visitor's chair and give me a run-down on my daughter.

"Emmy ate a whole egg for breakfast this morning," she

reported. "She slept almost eleven hours last night without waking up once."

That was big news. Emmy had always been a difficult sleeper. It brought a worry to my mind, though. "Do you think she's sleeping so much because she's had a head injury?" I asked.

"No, honey, she was thoroughly checked out by Dr. Martin in the E.R. and then again in his office the next day. She has some bruises from where her car seat restraints held her, but that's all. That car seat was the best investment ever," Mom said with a touch of smugness.

Mom and Dad had gotten the car seat for Emmy before she was born, spending a horrific amount of money on it, and then had the guys at the car shop install it properly in my back seat. Dad said if I was going to drive a little tin can of a car, he'd at least try to keep his granddaughter safe. As usual, he was right. And thank God he was.

"I hear you're being released tomorrow," Mom said. She knew more about that than I did, having met her old friend, Dr. Martin, in the hall. "Of course, you'll come home."

Of course. There could be no question of my returning to my upstairs apartment toting a heavy two-year-old. I'd already figured that out.

"Your room is just the way you left it," Mom continued. "Except Emmy's crib is in there now. So you girls will be just snug as bugs. And Dad and I will be right there to help with Emmy."

That was nothing new. They'd both been helping with Emmy since I got the job at the bank. I wondered what would happen to that job now. It had been quite a coup – for my father, that is. I needed to work, but had neither skills nor experience to offer a potential employer. However, Dad and the president of the bank were old buddies, and Dad reminded him that I'd gotten good grades in school, especially in math. Next thing I knew, I was a teller-in-training at First Bank of Butte. I didn't hate it, but I didn't love it, either. The salary would keep the lights on in my apartment, but no way would it stretch to cover day care. That's where my folks came in. Actually, they came in much more than I'd have liked, but beggars can't be choosers.

Now I wondered: even with my special "good old boy" hook-up, how long would the bank hold the job for a new hire not even finished with her training? Did the accident mean I'd be returning permanently to my parents' home, Emmy in tow, wiping out the hard-won independence of the past year?

I settled in at Mr. Jacoby's house, placing my meager belongings in the closet and the bureau drawers. The furniture was large and dark, but the private bathroom had a warming rail for towels and a tub big enough to water horses. It looked a lot more comfortable than anywhere I'd been sleeping lately. I snuggled into the wide bed and passed out.

When the alarm clock announced that it was six-thirty the next morning, I rolled out of bed immediately and ducked into the shower. Didn't want to be late my first morning. Awake and revived, I went to Mr. Jacoby's room to help him get ready for the day.

I knocked on his door before opening it and calling out, "Good morning." A cascade of barks answered me, and a little brown dog jumped down from the bed and came over to give me a thorough sniffing. I reached down, ruffled the silky ears and was rewarded by a wet kiss on the hand.

My mind flew back over the years to my childhood dog, Chummy. I'd loved that dog. Then one day when I came home from school, Chummy wasn't there to greet me with her mad, happy dance. Dad said she'd gone to live on a farm, that she'd be happier there. Like she'd packed her little suitcase and called a cab. End of story. I didn't dare ask any more, and I knew the futility of crying in front of my father. But I knew Chummy wouldn't be happier without me, nor would I be happy without her. Much as I liked dogs, I'd never had another one. Too risky.

The room was in darkness. As my eyes adjusted, I saw an inert shape under the bedcovers. Oh, God, don't tell me he's dead on my first day.

But the shape stirred and a hoarse voice said, "Good morning, John. You're up early."

"It's seven. That's when you said you wanted to get up, right?"

"That's right. I've been awake for hours, or maybe not totally awake, drifting in and out of sleep. My back's killing me."

Mr. Jacoby struggled to sit up and swing his feet over the side of the high bed. I crossed quickly to him and held out my arm like a grab-bar.

"Here, hold onto my arm," I said. "Okay, now get your feet on the floor. Take your time. Rock back and forth a couple of times to get some momentum going, then lean forward and push up with your heels. On three: one, two, three – up you go."

Gasping, he was on his feet, but I could feel his unsteadiness through the arm he held. "Let's just stand here a minute," I said. "Get your bearings."

What was the rehab place thinking, letting this guy go home? How he'd ever gotten out of bed and dressed by himself was a mystery. He definitely needed help.

We shuffled to the bathroom, where he asked that I wait outside while he urinated. It took a while. When he opened the door he'd already begun to remove his pajamas. I busied myself with getting the shower temperature just right. When I turned back, Mr. Jacoby was standing there starkers, looking embarrassed and uncomfortable. Well, it didn't faze me, I've seen lots of naked old men, but I realized it was different for him. I didn't make eye contact as I helped him into the shower, trying to give him a little dignity through my detachment. It was a big, deep porcelain tub with a removable shower head above, so he had to make a big step over the side. I noted the absence of grab bars; I'd install them immediately. There was a portable plastic bench in the tub where he would sit while showering and that's what he was aiming for. He got one foot up and over, but as he raised the other leg, he lost his balance. I grabbed him around the waist, and found myself with my face pressed into his skinny ass as we maintained a precarious balance.

I felt him begin to shake. Was he having a seizure? I tried to shift my grip on his body, but he was slippery with the water that was beating down on both of us. I heard a strangled sound – was he choking? Then I realized he was laughing. The old coot was shaking with laughter, and in that moment, I realized how funny we must look. I started laughing, too, and somehow, we got him situated on the shower chair, despite our mutual guffaws.

"Oh my," he finally managed, "oh my, John, I guess you'd better call me Charles, now that we've developed such a close relationship."

For the rest of the day, whenever he caught my eye he'd chuckle. He wasn't embarrassed after that, no matter what kind of help he needed.

~*~

I knew I wasn't thinking clearly when Mom had to remind me about the man who pulled Emmy and me from the car. I should be thanking him up one side and down the other, but somehow it just hadn't occurred to me. What he did was heroic, far beyond what could reasonably be expected of a perfect stranger. Without him, Emmy and I wouldn't be here, or maybe we'd have survived but with awful injuries. So I needed to thank him. Of course I did. But my mind stopped there.

Mom, though, nothing stops her mind. She told me that the man – his name was John Carver, she said – was staying with Uncle Charles. That blew my mind. How did that happen? Granted, Charles needed more help than he was getting. He could depend on Grand Butte neighbors to look in on him – in fact, Emmy and I had been on our way to check on him when we had the accident. But how did this Carver guy get involved, and what qualified him to provide care? It was all too hard to figure out. My eyes closed.

When they opened again, Mom was sitting at my bedside, fizzing with excitement. She started right in.

"You'll never guess what," she said rhetorically. "The town is throwing a party for John Carver!"

If there's anything my mom loves, it's planning and executing a party. So when she said "the town", I knew what she really meant is "I."

"He has to stay on for a week waiting for a starter for his car," she continued. "And I was talking to Daw and Janie, and they just think the world of him, and now he's staying with Uncle Charles, and I thought we ought to do something to acknowledge his heroic act and thank him."

She paused and gave me a look, daring me to object. Parties are big in Grand Butte. It doesn't take much of a reason to throw one, and the whole town turns out. Mom loves them; I loathe them. But how could I object? The man saved our lives, mine and Emmy's.

"That sounds great, Mom," I said, trying to muster some enthusiasm. "Maybe I won't be able to go, though," I added hopefully.

"Of course you will," Mom said. "Dr. Mason is releasing you today. You'll have to take it easy for a while, but not so easy that you can't thank the man who saved your life. Come on, let's get you dressed and packed. There's a little girl at home waiting for you."

The thought of Emmy was enough to get me moving. I pictured her bright eyes and the scanty little pigtails I tie up with bows. Mom'd have her dressed in something fluffy and smocked, a cotton dress that needed expert ironing. I dressed her in pants and tee-shirts that went warm from the dryer onto her back. But that was all small stuff. My little girl wanted her mommy, that's what was important.

I didn't remember about the party until much later, after the hugs and games of peek-a-boo and who-hid-Honey-Bunny with Emmy, after eating more of Mom's dinner than I wanted, after laying my broken bones down with a groan between the smooth, lavender-scented sheets in my old bedroom. And by then, I was too exhausted to think for long. Tomorrow....

~*~

A party? I could definitely do without a party. These people didn't seem to have an inkling that a person might guard his privacy, might want to keep to himself. They were all about warm welcomes and huge thank-yous. I tried to dissuade Daw and Janie when they stopped by to check on Charles.

"Look, it's not necessary," I said. "I don't need to be publicly praised. It's enough to know that it turned out okay."

"Okay?" Janie looked incredulous. "John, you saved two lives that night. This is a small community. If Bree and Emmy had been killed in that wreck, we'd all be grieving. But thanks to you, they're alive, and we want to have a party. Bree's mom is planning it."

So a party there would be, and I'd put on my best public face for it. But I was filled with dread. People like me didn't have parties thrown for them. Well, lynching parties, maybe.

Charles said, "You deserve it, John." At my look of disbelief, he said, "Yes, you do. Accept that you are the focus of a great deal of gratitude. Soak it up."

"But I don't deserve it," I mumbled. At that moment, I wanted to tell him everything. It would have been such a relief to unload my secret, let someone else carry a tiny piece of it for me. But I knew if that genie ever exited the bottle, I'd have to leave town the same day.

I'm stuck here until my car is fixed, I reminded myself. Once I can leave, I'll just slip away with no good-byes. I'll be forgotten before my taillights fade from view. And so I bit back my urge to confide in Charles. People shouldn't be so darn trusting.

~*~

Mom was in full, manic, party mode. If Dad hadn't been around to help me with Emmy, I don't know how I'd have managed. Broken ribs and a toddler saying, "Up, up" don't mix well. My foot was in a walking boot, and I could get around okay in the house. But those ribs! Like stilettos, they stabbed my chest when I moved or did my breathing exercises. The doctor assured me they were healing, that it was a slow process and I'd just have to be patient.

With Mom chasing around planning the party, it was left to Dad to bathe Emmy, take her for walks, swing her up into her highchair and supervise her outdoors. I sat on the sofa surrounded by the detritus of illness: half-full glass of water, box of tissues, books and television remote. I could cuddle

Emmy there on the sofa, read her stories and watch endless cartoons with her. That was about it.

"The bank called," Dad said on the second day I was home. "They're holding your job." He sounded pleased with himself, and I knew he'd reached out again to his buddy, the bank president.

"But how long can they keep it open?" I asked. "It feels like I'll never get back to normal."

"Of course you will," Dad said. "What did the doctor say about patience?"

"Yeah, I know. It's hard, though. I want to go home."

"You are home, Bree," Dad said. "This will always be your home."

So my parents had their daughter back, and better yet, their granddaughter. The blessed privacy of my own little apartment seemed like a dream that vanished upon waking.

Meanwhile, Mom was bugging me about what I'd be wearing to the party.

"It'll have to be something loose that buttons in front," I said. "I can't raise my arms."

She returned from her next round of errands with a "couple little things she'd picked up." A white blouse with delicate embroidery around the hem, black pants, a full-length caftan, light as a feather, that she assured me we could easily slip over my head, and a short dress.

"But I'd recommend either the blouse and pants or the caftan, so your walking boot won't show," Mom said.

"I'm pretty sure everybody would love to see my walking boot," I replied, "but they'll probably be satisfied with looking at my facial bruises."

Arriving at the town hall, we saw that the parking lot was full. Mom commandeered a handicapped space despite my protests that we didn't have the requisite permit and that I could walk from a more distant space.

"Nonsense," she said briskly. "Who is more handicapped than you right now? And who's going to write a ticket – Daw?"

Dad carried Emmy and Mom held my arm. When we walked in the door, we saw all our friends and neighbors. There was a predictability to these affairs. The women of the town cooked and baked, bringing in their special dishes for a pot-luck supper. The men brought the booze and mixers, the ice chests filled with beer and soft drinks. Everyone knew Janice would make her potato salad, Ernie would buy a case of Bud Lite, and Carolyn's blackberry cobbler would be front and center on the dessert table. Once I'd found it all mind-numbingly boring, but now I was touched by the efforts made just because they were glad Emmy and I were still around.

Uncle Charles shuffled over in his walker and embraced me carefully, minding my ribs. Then he motioned to the man at his side and said, with his old-fashioned courtesy, "Bree, may I present John Carver. John, this is Bree and her daughter, Emmy. You may remember them from your earlier encounter."

"How do you do?" I said, influenced by Uncle Charles' beautiful manners.

John looked like somebody had just smacked him. He didn't speak, just stared at me.

"I need to thank you," I said, feeling self-conscious under his gaze. "You risked your life to save Emmy and me."

"No problem," John mumbled. I saw him make an effort to stop staring at me.

Uncle Charles moved smoothly into the little pause, shooing

26

us to a table. I tried to relax and ignore John's silent regard. He was the big hero of the evening; he should concentrate on taking his bows.

~*~

I knew I was staring at Bree, but I couldn't seem to stop. She looked nothing like the person I'd pulled from the car. Her face then had been covered with blood from the cut on her forehead. Now I saw it was a distinctive face, pretty despite the row of sutures on her forehead and two black eyes. If she could look good with all that going on, she must be a knock-out at her best. Not that it mattered what she looked like. All that mattered was just her.

She carried herself tentatively, and I remembered she'd broken some ribs and her foot. I hurried to pull out her chair and help her get seated. I assisted Charles into the chair beside her, stowing his walker out of the line of traffic, and sat down on Bree's other side. Before I could get too panicked about the need for making conversation, Daw stepped up to a microphone, producing ear-splitting screeches and general laughter. He stepped back and grinned.

"I'm not going to take that personally," he said, gesturing at the mike. "We're here tonight to celebrate the lives of two of our own, and to express our appreciation to the man who saved them. John Carver was just driving down the road when he came upon a terrible scene, a car hanging half off a steep embankment with two people trapped inside. With no thought for his own safety, he chose to become involved, to do what he could to save those passengers. Folks, it takes a certain kind of person to have the presence of mind, the courage, to react in a crisis. John, please stand up."

I stood, feeling like a fool, my face hot. Daw continued.

"We're a pretty ingrown bunch here in Grand Butte, and most of the time we like it that way. But every now and then we get a visitor that makes us sit up and take notice. You might not think we have much use for keys since most of us don't even lock our doors, but... John, come on up here. I want to present you with the key to the city."

Daw held out a large, gilt key with one hand and extended the other hand for a handshake. I took both, grinning self-consciously.

"Uh, thanks, Daw, and thanks, everyone. I'm glad I could be of some help."

I ducked back into my seat, everyone applauded, and that seemed to be that. They turned back to their supper plates, and I turned to Bree. She smiled sympathetically and said, "Not easy being a hero, is it?"

John Carver wasn't at all what I expected. He was tall and strongly built, but carried himself with none of the confidence of a big man. Instead of expanding under the spotlight of approval, he seemed to shrink, to try to take up as little space as possible. I like a humble person as much as anyone else, but this seemed more like fear than modesty. I wondered what he was afraid of. Then there was his intense gaze, under which I felt like shrinking myself. I made an effort to engage him in small talk, trying to dilute that steady ray of attention.

"So, John. Where were you headed when you had the bad luck to come upon my accident?"

"Uh, nowhere in particular, I guess," he said. "I was just driving, figured I'd know where to stop when I saw it."

That intrigued me. It sounded like something Billy and I would have done, back in the day. "No job, no home or family?" I asked.

"No. Not even a dog," John said.

"Interesting. And yet somehow, you're now taking care of my Uncle Charles," I said, as I was reminded that raising my eyebrows hurt.

"Yeah. But that's just a temporary gig. He won't need my help very long, and the starter for my car should be coming in any day now."

"And then what?"

"Then, I don't know. My future is, well, unpredictable," John said, and finally took his gaze from my face, looking down.

Obviously this was not a subject he wanted to pursue. I could respect that. I wasn't so sure about my future, either.

Across the room, I saw Billy's parents. They glanced away quickly when they saw me looking. You'd think they'd be at least a little bit interested in how their granddaughter was doing, but the Ketchums showed no such interest. I guess they were concerned about possible consequences for Billy if they acknowledged Emmy, so they avoided contact. I was surprised they'd even showed up. But maybe I was being unkind. What is the proper protocol when your son knocks up a local girl and then takes off for parts unknown?

John was asking me a question. I tuned back in.

"Tell me about your little girl," he said. "We are sort of acquainted, but I hope she never remembers the wreck."

"She won't," I reply, "She's only two. But you can be sure she'll be hearing the story."

John looked uncomfortable. "I'm not asking for praise," he said. "Just wondered what your kid is like."

What mother could resist an opening like that? "Well, she's hell on wheels right now, constantly on the move and you have to keep up with her because she has no sense at all, not one little smidgeon. So she might stick her finger in a socket, walk off the top step, or pull down a tablecloth full of dishes over her head. It's exhausting, but she makes me laugh twenty times a day, and melts me just by saying 'Mama.'"

"Her father?" John asked.

"Isn't in the picture," I said briefly.

# Chapter Three

That was good news. I'd had to screw up my courage to ask, but the information that Emmy's daddy wasn't around was worth it. Despite the intensity of my feelings, I had no reason to think the attraction was anything but one-sided. Still, I was glad to know Bree was single.

Emmy was struggling to escape from her grandfather's grasp. I watched them across the table as he tried to engage Emmy's interest in his car keys, the silverware, the toy that Grandma pulled from her purse – nothing doing. The little girl wanted down, and that was a word she could and did say, loud and clear. Finally, he gave up and set her feet on the floor. Like the Road Runner, legs spinning, she took off. People at other tables laughed and reached out for her as she ran by. She seemed to feel perfectly comfortable in the crowded room, and I was reminded that this was a place where everyone knew everyone, even the babies.

Bree pushed back her chair and limped after her daughter, talked and laughing with people as she followed Emmy. There was a noticeable hush in the room when the little girl approached one table. Everyone looked at the couple sitting there. They bowed their heads, but the woman raised her eyes for just a second. I was struck by the look of longing on her face. The little girl kept going and the moment passed.

Bree caught Emmy's hand and led her back to our table. She resumed her seat and gingerly settled Emmy on her lap. Her mother handed over a storybook and Bree began showing Emmy the pictures. I watched their profiles bent over the book.

When Emmy began to squirm to get down again, I offered to walk her around a bit, and Bree let me. The tiny hand in mine was a new sensation. Emmy pulled me from Point A to Point B, using baby geography to chart our course. As we walked, people reached out to pat her and to shake my hand. I got a picture of what life in this small town must be like for those who belonged here. Forget it, John, I told myself sternly. This can never be yours.

When most people had finished their meals, there was a general shuffling around the room. Groups formed and reformed as neighbors caught up with neighbors. Many of them made their way over to me. The men slapped me on the back and some of the women hugged me. One middle-aged lady, who introduced herself as Bree's second-grade teacher, teared up a little as she told me what a dear child Bree had been, and how much she looked forward to teaching Emmy in a few years.

"If not for you, we might very well have lost these two. You showed true courage that night," she said, wringing my hand.

The minister of the church where Bree's family went took his time telling me the story of the Good Samaritan and drawing wholly unjustified parallels between that saintly person and me. I squirmed. He saw how uncomfortable I was.

"No, you deserve to be praised," he said. "You saved their lives, and now you're taking care of Charles. We see your kindness and courage, and we appreciate you."

I didn't know what to say. I felt overwhelmed. Would this evening never end? I looked for Charles and saw him hanging between the handles of his walker, looking exhausted. Gratefully, I made my way over to him and whispered, "Had enough? Ready to go home?"

"I'm a bit tired," he admitted, "but I don't want to cut this evening short for you."

"No worries," I said, steering him toward the door. Bree saw us heading out and waved. Emmy's head was drooping against her shoulder and it looked like it wouldn't be long before she'd be going home, herself. The party began to break up, and there were still more hugs and handshakes as people took their leave. Charles beamed as I fielded their good wishes as best I could.

Later that night, stretched out in my bed, hands behind my head, I reviewed the evening in my mind. These were nice people; that was evident. They couldn't have been more welcoming. Apparently, they had no inkling of stranger-danger. Daw hadn't even run my name through the criminal data-base. Part of me felt angry that they were so naïve and trusting. Didn't they watch the evening news? But a bigger part of me yearned for acceptance and basked in the warmth of their welcome. It had been a long time since I'd felt accepted. I knew it might never happen again. I thought I'd made peace with that. But now there was Bree.

~*~

Emmy was exhausted; it was long past her bed-time. Dad carried her into the house and she hardly stirred as I slipped her out of her clothes and into her pajamas. Only recently had it become unnecessary to add a night diaper. My little girl was growing up. I tucked the blanket around her and turned on the night light.

In the kitchen, Mom and Dad were having a cup of decaffeinated tea and reviewing the evening. After the usual critique of the food brought and consumed, they started on John Carver.

"I like him," my dad said. "He's got a good handshake. Quiet guy, doesn't blow his own horn."

"I thought he seemed uncomfortable with all the attention" Mom said. "Humility is a fine trait in a person. What did you think of him, Bree?"

"He's nice enough, and good with Uncle Charles; that's a big plus. But he's kind of a mysterious guy. He just appeared and will soon disappear without us knowing anything about him. He's very close-mouthed about his past and his future plans."

"I think he likes you," Mom said with an arch smile.

Uh-oh. Last thing I need is Mom getting into match-maker mode.

"Yeah, well, I'm not interested," I said.

"Bree, you need to move on," Mom said. "Your thing with Billy is over. He hasn't even contacted you once since he left to go into the service. He's not come home on leave, he's not sent a message through his parents. And as for his parents! Well! To not even acknowledge our sweet Emmy!"

This was a subject Mom could really get her teeth into. Despite the fact she didn't like Billy's family, didn't think he was good enough for me, and didn't want him on the scene as Emmy's daddy, she was outraged by the Ketchum's rejection of their only granddaughter.

To derail her, I let my shoulders slump. "I think I'm ready for bed," I said, realizing how much I meant it. My ribs were aching and the bones in my foot felt like they were on fire.

Mom immediately began bustling around, feeling my forehead, asking if I wanted a pain pill and if she should run a hot bath. I shook my head, waved goodnight and tiptoed into my old room, now shared with Emmy. Despite my exhaustion, sleep didn't come right away. Pictures from the evening parade through my mind: the curious, kind faces of my friends and neighbors, the genuine warmth of their welcome for John Carver, Emmy's toddling walk with her hand in his. What would it be like to have a father for my child? Secretly, I agreed with Mom that Billy would never be that person.

I'd been determined not to call him after he left. If he didn't care enough to even say goodbye, I sure as hell wasn't going to go running after him. I did write him a letter informing him of Emmy's birth. She was his child, too, after all. Since I didn't have his address, I left it with Mrs. Ketchum to send on. Maybe she hadn't done it. Maybe he still didn't know he – we – had a child. But that was on him. I mean, he had a cell phone; he could have called any time. Even if he didn't know about the baby, wouldn't he have wanted to explain why he'd enlisted, have asked me to wait for him? The Billy I knew and loved would have. This other Billy, the one who left without a word, was someone I didn't know.

The last image in my mind before sleep finally came was John Carver's face .

~*~

So now I had a problem. I needed to be gone, but I wanted to stay. Charles still required my help, but he was regaining strength and balance rapidly. In a matter of days, my car would be fixed, I'd collect my week's wages and it would be time to go. But how could I drive away from the possibilities that Bree represented?

I gave myself sensible pep-talks. Bree barely knows you; she has no feelings for you. You have nothing to offer her. She has her life and her child, her secure place in this world; she doesn't need a rolling stone like you. Your safest option is to keep moving, pick up odd jobs here and there, and put down no roots. Sure, Grand Butte people are welcoming now, but if they knew, if they ever found out about what happened, that would change in a New York minute.

The prison chaplain had counseled me to get on with my life, to let the past remain in the past, but I'd found it wasn't possible. There is one crime that never leaves, like the stain on the permanent record teachers used to scare us with. Only this crime really is permanent because a felony conviction will follow me all the days of my life. Google maps will track my whereabouts to warn neighbors that in their midst lives a predator. A pedophile.

It didn't matter what the extenuating circumstances were. I'd never have the chance to explain I didn't know Sue was only fifteen. She looked older. She said she was eighteen, my age at the time. I was crazy in love, as only teenagers can be. Sue supplied the warmth I'd longed for all my life; warmth that my parents had been incapable of providing. I had no self-restraint when it came to her and she was always ready and willing. We were together every possible minute. With her parents both at work, the house was ours during the day, and we took advantage of it with long afternoons in her little twin bed.

Her father came home from work unexpectedly one day, the victim of a bout of flu, and caught us there. He grabbed me and threw me bodily out of the house, flinging my clothes after me. Then he called the police. That's when I learned Sue's real age. Charges were pressed. Statutory rape. My public defender was fresh out of law school, only a few years older than I. He tried, but I drew the toughest judge on the

Texas bench, the kind who liked to make examples. "Four years," he said, adding a stern warning that by the time I got out, I'd be twenty-two and I'd better be wiser. Four years to serve, and a lifetime to regret.

Prison. I kept my head down, but a new inmate always causes arguments and violence. My conviction as a child molester meant a contingent of inmates would eventually find an opportunity to beat me up, maybe kill me. I had been convicted of one of the few crimes that other prisoners found unacceptable, and they weren't interested in hearing about the circumstances. Everybody in prison can tell a convincing story of innocence.

Meanwhile, some of the old cons fought over whose bitch I would be. I lived in fear. My cellmate wasn't interested in me, for which I thanked all the gods that be. He was old and had long ago withdrawn from the misery around him. He left me alone, but time in the shower and exercise yard with the other guys was like walking a tightrope over a den of hungry lions.

Our warden was reputed to be progressive, and maybe he was looking out for me because I was so young. I don't know. But rather than the usual laundry or kitchen assignments which would have left me at the mercy of the other inmates, I was assigned to the infirmary for my work detail. It was an oasis for me. I could shower there in peace, eliminating at least one hazardous situation from my day.

The infirmary doctor, Etienne Cambrone, was a good guy and kept a close eye on his few inmate workers. He was Haitian, had taken his medical training at the University of Haiti, and then come to the States thinking he could establish a practice. But his offshore medical degree wasn't enough for the credentialing officials in the large hospitals to which he applied for privileges. He needed to pass American medical boards, and he needed a way to earn a paycheck while he studied for them. So he took a job in the prison system, where standards weren't as exacting. Dr. Cambrone wasn't the type to put in his time and collect his pay. He gave his job all he had, and expected me to do the same. I was thankful every day for my prison assignment and decided to learn all I could from him while I had the opportunity.

Men who grow old in prison are subject to the same ailments as any old men. Although I was many years younger, I found I empathized with them. I assisted with bathing, spoon-fed the truly feeble and cleaned up after the confused. The most hardened criminals were grateful for any small kindnesses I could provide – a hot shower, an ice pack, a clean bed. It made me feel useful, like I was doing something that made a difference. I'd wondered, pre-prison, about a career in healthcare. That door was closed to me now, along with so many others. But I did like the work.

"You're a natural," Dr. Cambrone said in his lilting island accent, flashing his bright, white smile. We saw that smile a lot. He was unfailingly good-natured, even about his instant nickname, Papa Doc. "I hated Duvalier," he said with a shrug, "but I know the guys don' mean anything by it."

Papa Doc was kind to me when my elderly parents died, one after the other within a year of my incarceration. He listened patiently to stories of my childhood that I somehow had to get off my chest.

I knew I'd always been a source of confusion to my parents. They didn't know what to do with a lively boy who dropped unexpectedly into their late middle age. They coped as well as they could, but they'd never wanted a child. They frequently looked at me in surprise, as if I was a stranger who'd wandered into their house. I guess I was, really.

No matter how hard I tried, I couldn't break through that wall of detachment. Straight-A report cards, school awards, sports trophies all fell flat when I took them proudly to my folks.

"Hmmm," was the usual comment, followed by a turning away, a change of subject.

If it hadn't been for our neighbor, Sam – "Call me Sam, none of this mister business" – I wouldn't have known there could be a warm relationship with an adult. Sam loved me and he showed it. He hugged me every time he saw me, which was daily because I went to his house after school rather than going home. He'd have two glasses of milk and some store-bought cookies ready and we'd have a snack while I told him about my day. He knew the names of all my teachers, my best friends and worst enemies. Homework was done at his kitchen table, with Sam professing amazement at my grasp of math. "I just don't know how you do it," he'd say. "Why, my stars, integers! Whoever ever heard of such a thing?" I'd feel my chest expand with importance, and worked hard to bring him a test marked with an A.

Sam lived his days in a wheelchair, but somehow it was part of him and I didn't give it a second thought. I liked to do things for him: climbing up on a kitchen step-stool to get things down from the top cupboards; helping him tug on his compression stockings, which always made us hilarious at the sheer difficulty of it. Somehow his skinny, blue-veined legs just looked normal to me. He never spoke of being ill, and I had no idea of the serious health problems he faced. When he died during my junior year of high school, I was devastated. He left a hole in my life and my heart. Maybe that's why I was so crazy about Sue – she made me feel less alone. But later, after my arrest and conviction, I was glad he didn't live to see my disgrace. It might have been too much even for Sam.

It certainly was too much for my parents. Although we hadn't been close, I felt overwhelmed with guilt that the stress of having me in their lives had hastened their deaths. They left me a small savings account, just a few thousand dollars, and the house where I grew up. When I was released from prison, I turned the house key over to a property management company, instructed them to find a tenant and deposit the rent checks in an escrow account to handle expenses.

I'd chosen to serve my entire sentence rather than applying for parole so that when I got out, that chapter of my life was over. I wouldn't have to check in with a parole officer. I could leave. Now there was nothing to keep me in that neighborhood, enduring the stares and whispers of people who knew all about me. I cashed in the savings account, used the money to buy the first car I saw, and hit the road. My plan was to keep moving, but now I was here in Grand Butte, celebrated as a hero, homeless, keeping a crippling secret, and falling in love with a girl and a town. How I wanted to stay. How impossible that was.

The days seemed endless. There's not much you can do with broken bones except wait for them to knit. I could get around in the walking boot, but if I stood very long my foot flamed. Emmy moved like a flash and my poor father chased her because I couldn't. I watched from the couch and thought about my life.

Everything changed when I found out Billy'd left me pregnant with his child. What a cliché! My face burned when I remembered I'd always considered myself smarter than the average bear, only to fall into the oldest trap of all. My folks had been surprisingly calm about it. Just sighed. I guess they'd been expecting the news for years.

So, no New York, no job waiting tables, no groovy loft. Just more Grand Butte, more girlhood bedroom, and much more belly. People in town figured it out pretty quickly, even though I stayed at home as much as possible. They were kind, because people in Grand Butte are kind, but I felt detached from them, and from everything. My high school girlfriends came around sometimes, but what did we have to talk about? They were off to college or working at their first jobs. I was sitting around the house getting as big as one. I drifted through the days.

The thing is, when you're pregnant, you can't drift for long because the baby is coming, ready or not. My parents assembled all the gear, including the car seat that would save her life one day. My second-grade teacher, Mrs. Willett, broke through my lethargy by proposing that she throw me a baby shower. I said, "Absolutely not." No way was I going to endure an evening of everyone being very kind about my predicament, just to rake in a few baby clothes. But Mom insisted it would be the height of bad manners to refuse, and I finally gave in, too disheartened to fight about it.

You know how you have that one special teacher? Mrs. Willett was mine. She was one of the few who didn't constantly summon my parents to school to talk about my wicked ways. Mrs. Willett understood I couldn't sit still. She let me roam when I needed to move. She gave me interesting books when she saw I'd been reading for some time and that Dick and Jane just weren't cutting it for me. When I grew into a rebellious teen, she always made a point of speaking to me on the street. She'd been determined to stick by one of her more difficult students, and she was still at it. Thus, the shower.

On that evening, I pulled my hair back in a ponytail and put on my maternity jeans with the stretchy panel and the biggest top I had. I wished for an invisibility cloak. Mrs. Willett's living room looked like a nursery explosion had happened in there. Pink and blue paper chains swagged over the curtains. There was a bowl of pink punch with blobs of sherbet floating in it. A large layer cake on a raised stand looked impressive. The icing said, "Welcome Baby." She'd even gotten out those little clear glass plates with matching cups – hostess sets, they were called – used only for special occasions.

The chairs along the walls were filled with my old school-mates and many of their mothers. All the faces turned to me when I entered the room, and every one of them smiled. I was enveloped in hugs, and my tummy was patted fondly. The prevailing mood was that I was in for a wonderful experience, and they all wanted to share in it. I looked into their eyes searching for sneers, but I saw only affection and good will.

That evening changed something in me. Grand Butte, provincial, back-water, insular, deadly-dull Grand Butte, was filled with people who cared about me. They genuinely wished me well. They welcomed my baby, regardless of the circumstances of her arrival. This was where we belonged. It was our safe haven. Once I'd wanted nothing more than to leave; now I felt I never would.

Charles was getting stronger every day. He negotiated the shower with ease now, while I waited outside the bathroom door. We both grinned when we remembered that first shower.

I'd taken him out for a drive, and he'd delighted in pointing out the local sights and telling me the history of each one.

"Have you always lived here?" I asked.

"My entire life," he said. "Born and raised. My father started the first bank and my mother taught Latin in the high school. The only time I've been away for any length of time was my stint in the Army. They sent me to Korea for a year. Well, I've traveled a bit, of course. Europe, what little I saw of Asia when I was stationed there, and one trip to Australia. I didn't have a wife to nag me to get up and go, and I found it easier to stay at home most of the time."

"Do you regret not having traveled more?" I asked.

"Not a bit," he said. "I love it here. This is where my roots are and where I feel the most like myself."

"It seems like a great place," I said, hearing the wistfulness in my own voice.

"Do you think so?" Charles said. "It's a funny old town – not for everyone. Folks aren't too interested in what goes on in the outside world. There's a great closeness and loyalty here. It can be stifling if it doesn't suit your personality. Maybe all small towns are the same. Was your home town like that, too?"

"No," I said shortly. He saw that I was uncomfortable, and with his usual tact, changed the subject.

The days seemed long, but they passed peacefully enough. I walked the dog, whose name was Queenie, and who had decided she liked me very much. I liked her, too. One day Charles asked me to take him to meet his friends for lunch at the same diner I'd camped in front of on my first night in town. There, I nursed several cups of coffee and waited while Charles laughed and talked with his buddies. He invited me to join them with his usual graciousness, and they were all cordial and welcoming, but I told him I'd prefer to wait for him, to go ahead and enjoy himself. Watching him over the book I'd brought along, I wondered what it must feel like to have friends as close as brothers. Or to have brothers, for that matter.

The phone call from Doug at the garage finally came a week to the day after my car broke down. "Car's fixed," he said laconically. "I'll run it by this afternoon."

Charles looked sad, but nodded when I told him. "Of course, it's time for you to be on your way," he said. "You never meant this to be a destination, I understand that. I'll be fine now. You've been a great help, and Queenie and I will miss you. You're welcome to stay on longer if you want."

I reached down and ruffled Queenie's ears. I'd miss them, too, but I'd decided the only sane thing for me to do was make the break now, before it got any harder. There was no future for me with Bree Carrolton, no matter how much I wished it. I could wait until she knew the truth about me and I got chased out of town in disgrace, or I could leave now with what remained of my dignity.

"Thanks, Charles," I said, "but I'd better be moving on. It's been great here and you've been so kind, but...."

"Of course," he said again. "Do you want to say goodbye to anyone? Daw and Janie? Bree?"

"No, I think it would be better if I just ease on down the road," I said. Actually, I wanted to see Bree again more than anything, but I knew it would make it even harder to go.

He went to his desk and wrote out a check for more than the figure he'd originally named, which had been very generous. He waved away my protests.

"You've earned it," he said, "for putting up with me with such kindness. I hope we can keep in touch."

Charles rubbed his temples as he spoke. I noticed how tired he looked.

"Do you have a headache?" I asked. Something about the way he looked made my antenna go up.

"Just... Yes, a small one," he said. "Maybe I'll have a little nap, sleep it off."

I went upstairs to pack my few belongings, leaving Charles stretched out on the sofa under a blanket. When I returned, suitcase in hand, he was snoring in a way that sounded almost like strangling. I touched his shoulder, but he didn't twitch. When I shook him gently his eyes fluttered open, but he had trouble keeping them open.

"Charles?" I said. "Are you okay?"

He struggled to sit up and that's when I noticed the wet spot beneath him. I grasped his shoulders and helped him sit upright, but he listed to the right.

"Charles, hold your arms out straight in front of you."

He tried, but the right arm drifted downward.

"Smile at me," I ordered.

Only one side of his mouth turned up.

"Can you tell me how you're feeling?" I asked, fearing the answer.

"Nobush letle," he said, looking confused and anxious. "Ich bogle truvy?"

"We need to get you to a hospital. I'm going to call an ambulance now. You sit tight," I said.

Charles's eyes were closing again. I dialed 911.

# Chapter Four

We heard about Charles' stroke as we were sitting down to dinner. Mom got up from the table, grabbed her car keys and went out the door in one motion, leaving Dad and me with our mouths open. She called after she'd spoken to the doctor.

"He's had a major stroke," she said. "Dr. Martin wants him to go back to the rehab place, but when he said that to Charles, the poor old thing actually cried. He can't speak right now, but his tears said it all. He's already spent two months in that place. He doesn't want to go back."

Mom said John was leaving, practically had one foot out the door when he realized Uncle Charles was having a stroke. He'd gotten Charles to the hospital and the vital dose of tPA that would make all the difference in his recovery.

John was leaving? Just like that? I thought we'd have a chance to become friends, but he'd been leaving without so much as a goodbye. I seemed to bring that out in guys.

"Dad, can you watch Emmy for an hour?" I asked. "And can I

borrow your car? I'm going to go see John Carver." I barely waited for his nod before I was gone.

I found him in the emergency department waiting area. Uncle Charles was being transferred to a hospital room and John said he wanted to know he was settled before he left.

"What's going to become of him?" I asked.

"He should make a good recovery," John said. "Luckily, we got here well within the three hour treatment window. It'll take a while to relearn speech and strengthen his right side, but I think he'll do well. He's a tough old guy."

"He doesn't want to go back to the rehab place," I said.

John nodded. "Can't blame him. He's been there, done that."

"But he can't be home alone," I added, looking at him searchingly.

"No," John said, meeting my eyes.

"Would you – can you stay with him?" I asked.

"Do you want me to?" John asked.

"I do. If you can. Please."

"Then I will."

I went to Uncle Charles' house every day after he was released from the hospital. John had his hands full, because Charles seemed to have undergone a personality change. The sweet nature I'd known all my life had morphed into a stubbornness, an emotionality, that made him seem like a stranger at times.

"He does that," John said quietly the first time I saw Uncle Charles burst into tears because he couldn't find the words he wanted to say. "He's weak, and his brain has been damaged, so he gets frustrated. Charles, let's walk a little bit."

Tenderly, the young man helped the old man to his feet and took his arm. "Let's go outside, okay?"

"Don' wanna!" Charles said loudly, pulling away.

"Come on, Uncle Charles," I said, slipping my arm through his. "Will you go outside with me?"

"Sure, honey," Charles said distinctly, beaming his still-lopsided smile at me.

Being outdoors soothed Charles' spirit, although he often resisted making the effort at first. But as long as I was at his side, he was amenable to suggestions. And so I went daily, sometimes bringing Emmy, sometimes waiting until she was napping. John and I developed a camaraderie as we plotted ways to get Uncle Charles to do his exercises, to interact verbally and to eat more than a couple bites.

I didn't miss the look on John's face whenever I arrived. I liked him, too, but the last thing I needed was a relationship, so I tried to keep our interactions on a friendly level. I was just there to help Uncle Charles get well. But secretly, I had to admit to myself John was a super guy. Maybe at another time, in another place...but here and now? No thanks, not interested.

There I was again, back in Charles' house, still in Bree's vicinity. Part of me was exultant, although the more sensible brain cells knew it was a bad idea. Still, Charles needed someone, and most of the time he liked and trusted me.

The stroke had changed him, but I believed that as its aftereffects wore off and more healing took place, he'd return to his old self. The tears, the irascibility, were not off-putting to me. Some of the old guys in prison had suffered strokes, and I'd seen it all before. The trick to handling them was unending patience and a tolerance for the monotony of repetition. Charles could learn only by repeating and repeating an action or a speech pattern. It was as if new grooves had to be made in his brain, as if it had been wiped clean. Strokes are unpredictable. In some undamaged corner of his mind, Charles retained his ability to read and write. He even used proper English when he was writing, although when he talked he used as few words as possible. Writing tired him, so we saved written communications for important things like medicine and symptoms. Otherwise, I learned to understand his garbled speech pretty well.

The physical therapist came every other day to put Charles through his paces. I watched as he carefully negotiated stairs, got up and down from chairs and climbed in and out of his high bed. Progress was slow, but discernible. Regaining his ability to speak clearly was harder. The speech therapist worked with him in her office twice a week. I took him for those visits. From my chair in the waiting room, I'd hear Charles' voice raised in frustration, then apology. His lovely manners were still in there somewhere, and surfaced when he realized he'd been rude to a lady. My heart went out to him as he struggled to find himself, but the last thing he needed was pity. Matter-of-fact cheerfulness and firm, tough love would get him through this.

Bree brought both. Her visits were the shining light in the tunnel of my days. Charles was a lamb with Bree. He brightened even more when she brought Emmy. The old man and the little girl never seemed to misunderstand each other, although they exchanged few words. She'd wrap her tiny hand around Charles' finger and off they'd go, pointing out interesting things to each other in a form of communication known only to them. Bree and I trailed behind. We exchanged small talk that gradually deepened into more meaningful exchanges. I heard stories of her growing-up years, and eventually, of Emmy's advent into her life. She spoke of her confusion over what to do next, now that she was a single mother with a child to support.

"What about Emmy's father – Billy, isn't it?" I asked. "Won't he help?"

"Doesn't look like it," she said. "Last I heard, he was in Afghanistan. It got around town that he spends his leaves traveling around Asia. After I heard that, I always envisioned him basking on a beach while I coped with teething and diaper rash. Not fair of me, he may not even know he has a child. And he's a soldier, he deserves his time off. But still…It's hard to reconcile that picture of him with the boy I knew. Loved."

"Loved? Past tense?"

"Yeah, I guess," Bree said, but she sounded doubtful.

~*~

It wasn't my idea to blow out of town like my hair was on fire. That was Daw and my dad, and they were motivated more by a mutual desire to get rid of me than any good wishes for my future. Daw said boosting the Congregationalist minister's car was the last straw. I returned it, but not before having a minor traffic accident. Just a dent or two, which wasn't bad considering how drunk I was. Daw persuaded the good man not to press charges on the condition that I leave town and stay gone. Somehow, he kept the whole thing quiet. I know I was a pain in the ass in those days and I guess I'd used up my lifetime supply of tolerance by then.

My biggest regret was leaving Bree without so much as a good-bye. There were a thousand opportunities to tell her what happened in between Daw's ultimatum and the day I left, but I didn't have the guts. Just went slinking off like a coward. We had so many plans, she and I, and it was hard to know we'd never get to fulfill them. I couldn't bear to see the love in her eyes replaced by hurt.

And yet, part of me was excited about joining the Army. The recruiter painted a rosy picture of travel and free education that was enticing to a kid with no prospects. I guess that's always been the lure of the Armed Forces. I meant to get in touch with Bree as soon as I got settled.

But then came boot camp and it was intense. Our cell phones were confiscated first thing so there'd be no tempting lifeline to home. Then a conceited small town Romeo got broken down systematically and rebuilt piece by piece. The drill sergeant took me completely out of my frame and made me into somebody new. After the initial shock, I became determined to excel and I worked harder than I'd ever worked in my life. I found I liked the structure and the discipline, felt proud to wear the uniform and be part of something bigger than myself. Before I knew it, three months had flown by and I was fit, trim and mentally tough.

I could have called her then, but it seemed too late. It would just be awkward, embarrassing. Her memory had faded, like something from another life. I told myself she'd moved on. Mom used to play a Frank Sinatra record where he sang, "It was great fun, but it was just one of those things." That's what it was, just one of those things. I didn't want to admit I didn't have the nerve to contact Bree. If anyone ever deserved a tongue-lashing it was me, and I knew she'd give me one. It was easier just to concentrate on the busy days of Army life and let thoughts of home recede. God, I was so young and stupid!

My first assignment was to Afghanistan, Kandahar province. The suffocating heat, the constant danger, the camaraderie with my brother soldiers filled my mind. I didn't write home much, and my folks weren't letter-writers themselves. There was no computer at their house for e-mails, and long-distance calls were still, in their minds, things to be feared and avoided.

When I went on leave, I explored the beaches of Thailand and Vietnam. The Asian girls were beautiful and some of them were willing to have a casual hook-up with an American soldier. At the end of the first year, I volunteered to stay on in Afghanistan, and again at the end of the second year. But now, three years into my enlistment, I felt homesick for the first time. Then I got a letter from Mom.

> Dear Son,
>
> How are you? I hope you are fine. We are all fine, except Blue died last week, but he was 12 and that's old for a coonhound. Dad buried him up under that cedar tree where he liked to rest.
>
> Dad doesn't know I am writing to you. He said not to, but I think you should know something. After you left, Bree turned up pregnant. She said it was your baby, but we weren't sure. Bree was wild, and we thought it could easily have been somebody else's. She had a girl she named Emmy. Dad said I should stay out of it and keep my mouth shut, so I did. But I see Bree and Emmy around town sometimes, and son, that baby looks just exactly like you did at the same age. I pulled out your baby pictures, and she's you made over. I believe Emmy is your daughter, and you have a right to know that. But don't say nothing to Dad that I wrote.
>
> Love, Mom

I put in for Stateside leave that same day.

~*~

I looked forward to my daily visits to Uncle Charles. I was easing back to work half-time, so I'd get off at noon. If it was one of the days Emmy declined to nap, a recent development,

I'd take her along. Sometimes we'd have a picnic lunch on the patio, where it didn't matter how messy Uncle Charles and Emmy were. He loved to see her and it seemed to do him good. Queenie frisked beside them as they took long, slow walks.

John and I had lots of time to talk and he was a good listener. I found myself pouring out the sad story of my life so far. I tried to be as honest and objective as possible. What happened to me was the result of decisions I made, and I didn't want to make myself out to be a victim. It was such a relief to get it off my chest, to tell it to someone who didn't already know, that I never noticed that John didn't reciprocate with his life story. I just thought he was a great confidant, non-judgmental and accepting.

John's kindness was not reserved only for me. He was patient and cheerful with Uncle Charles, no matter how ornery the old man got, and Emmy now ran to John for a hug the minute she saw him. A man who is kind to the sick and loved by a child…I began to appreciate John in a new way.

One day Uncle Charles was especially hard to handle. He'd not only refused his breakfast, but had actually knocked the bowl of oatmeal to the floor. Then he'd cried tears of frustration and shame. He'd resisted any attempts at distractions and sulked until I arrived after lunch. John whispered, "Look out, it's not been a good day so far."

We went outside into the sunshine, usually a cure for Charles' bad moods, but not this day. He ignored Emmy's tugging at his hand to walk with her, and settled sullenly into a double seated Adirondack chair. It's hard to feel sympathy for someone who is angry, and I found myself ignoring Charles. John, however, sat down beside him. He continued talking quietly to me and Emmy while edging closer to Charles until they were sitting shoulder-to-shoulder. John put an arm around him, gently rubbing his back. Eventually, Charles' face smoothed and he leaned back in the sunshine. When Emmy came back to beg for a walk, he rose and shuffled along with her.

"Sometimes they just need to be touched," John said to me. "Stroke victims feel alone and scared. Charles is doing well, but he can't always see it."

"How did you get to know so much about it?" I asked.

"Oh, I've worked in a hospital," John replied.

When he didn't elaborate, I persisted. "Where?"

"In another state," John said. He obviously didn't want to talk about it.

"Is that what you do for a living? Work in hospitals? Are you a nurse or a doctor?"

"None of the above," he said. "Just an orderly. I like the work, though."

"Have you thought of pursuing it professionally? Getting qualified in some way?" I asked.

"Wish I could. It's not likely. There are things you don't know about me, Bree."

"Do you want to tell me?"

"Not now. Not the right time."

Just then Uncle Charles and Emmy returned from their circuit of the garden, Emmy clutching a stone she was excited to show us. Our conversation was over, but my curiosity was piqued now. I wanted to know more. What was in John's past that wouldn't stand the light of day? I hoped it wasn't anything too bad.

~*~

I knew she'd back me into a corner sooner or later. She'd told me a lot about her life, and I'd told her nothing in return. She was bound to get curious. My mind was in turmoil for the rest of the day. Just as I'd felt we were becoming friends, and maybe a little bit more than friends, I came square up against the realization I was living in a fool's paradise. I knew I had to tell her. Better that she heard it now, from me, before things progressed any further. It would mean the end of our friendship, but I'd expected that all along. I hoped she'd let me stay on with Charles until he was better, but I was prepared to move on if she wouldn't.

That night, after I'd gotten Charles settled in bed to watch television until he grew drowsy, I went to his desk and looked up Bree's parents' phone number in his leather-bound address book. Bree'd never given me her cell phone number. Mrs. Carrolton answered the phone.

"Why, hello, John," she said cordially. "How are you this evening? Is everything all right with Charles?"

"Yes, Mrs. Carrolton. I didn't mean to alarm you. Charles is fine. He's turned in for the night. I wonder if I could speak with Bree."

"Of course, let me call her. Oh, and John: I want to say again how much I appreciate your staying on to care for Charles. I know you've put your own life on hold. Because of you, he's been able to stay in his own home and I believe it will speed his recovery."

"No problem. I like Charles a lot. He's been good to me."

"Let me get Bree for you," she said, and I heard her put the phone down.

"Hello?" Bree said a moment later.

"Bree, it's John. I wondered if you could come back to Charles' house this evening. I'd like to continue our conversation that got interrupted this afternoon."

"Now? I just put Emmy to bed. Let me see if my parents are going to be home tonight."

Another pause. I could hear the murmur of voices.

"Yes, okay, John, I'll come on over. Is something wrong?"

"I'll let you decide that after you've heard what I have to say."

I paced in circles until I heard the crunch of her tires on the gravel drive. Then I moved to the door to open it before she rang the bell. I didn't need Queenie barking and Charles calling out to know who was there. My face must have looked like doom, because Bree's smile died as she got a look at me. I led her into the den, where we took the chairs on either side of the fireplace. A fire might have made the setting cozier, but even without it, I was sweating. I took a deep breath and began.

Bree's eyes never left my face as I talked. When I ran out of words, she looked away, gazing out of the darkened window. I wondered what she was seeing. Finally, she spoke.

"So you were eighteen and Sue was fifteen," she said. "I can relate. I was fifteen when I fell in love with Billy. I know how love feels at that age. My dad once threatened to do exactly what Sue's father did – file statutory rape charges. He never did it, probably because he knew we would have just run away."

"But the circumstances were different, Bree," I said. I was determined not to give myself any kind of a pass, not with this girl. "I was old enough to have had better sense. I went to prison for what I did, and when I got out, I just ran. I was trying to put the greatest possible distance between me and the Texas prison system."

"Yet you stopped to help me and Emmy," Bree said.

"I never even thought about not stopping," I said.

57

Improbably, Bree started to laugh. "I'm just picturing Daw's face when he hears this," she said. "He apparently didn't do very good police work, or he'd have known about your record."

"I know. I've been waiting for the other shoe to drop. You going to tell him?"

"Me? No. Daw sent Billy away. If it hadn't been for him, Billy and I would be married and Emmy would have a Daddy. No, I won't be telling Daw anything. Let him do his own damn work."

"Do you hate me now?" I asked, too afraid of her answer to put the question any less baldly.

"Of course not," Bree said, looking surprised. "The way I see it, you got a harsh punishment for something that was only partly your fault. You've more than paid for some dumb moves you made when you were a kid. I've made a few dumb moves myself. Most people have."

"But what I did was beyond normal teenage mistakes. It was unforgiveable," I said. "It's part of me now. It is me."

"Is it?" Bree said. "Why are you determined to hang onto the worst version of yourself?"

I couldn't meet her eyes. The answer seemed so evident: because I deserved it.

"I read this somewhere," she continued. "Stand sideways in front of a full-length mirror and let your shoulders slump and your belly poke out. That's one version of you. Then stand up straight, suck in your gut and pull your shoulders back. Whole different picture, yet it's the same body, the same bones, the same muscles. It's all in how you choose to present yourself."

I digested that for a moment. She had a point, but it seemed impossible to let go of the image that had been drummed into me for the last four years.

"But what do you think your folks would say if they knew?" I persisted. "And the rest of the town? I really love it here, but I'd have to leave right away if they found out. Wouldn't I?"

"People would be concerned, for sure," Bree said thoughtfully. "If they knew the whole story, I think they'd give you a break, but the word 'pedophile' is so scary they might not wait to hear any more. The people in Grand Butte think you're a hero, so there'd be a lot of confusion. As a whole, folks around here are pretty tolerant, but I can't promise how far their tolerance would stretch."

"What do you think I should do?" I asked.

"Nothing, right now. Uncle Charles needs you, and that's got to be our main focus. Let's think about this for a few days," Bree said.

I felt a little better that she'd said "we." It was good to have an ally.

`

# Chapter Five

I wasn't as shocked by John's confession as a lot of people might have been. I'd spoken truly when I said I'd done my share of stupid things, and maybe I was less judgmental because of it. I wished I could help him shed his burden and see himself as I saw him, as the whole town saw him. But no matter how much you might want to rearrange the furniture in someone else's head, you can't. People only change when they're ready.

All thoughts of rescuing my rescuer fled, however, when my cell phone pinged at 3 AM with a message. Groggily, I reached for it and the print on the small screen lit up the darkness.

Bree, I didn't know about the baby. I'm coming home. Billy

I was mad as hell at my folks for not telling me. I'd been a father for two years and didn't know it. What gave them the right to judge Bree as they had? Because of them, she'd had to go through pregnancy and childbirth without me. Well, let's be honest: because of decisions I'd made, too. I wondered how she felt about me now. Too much time had passed for me to think, even at my most optimistic, that I could waltz back into her life. Being a mother had to have changed her. All I could do now was go and see.

The trip home by Army transport was a test of all the patience I never had. Droning along in the big troop plane, sitting on the vibrating steel floor eating MREs, all I could think of was hurry up, hurry up. But the Army hurries for no man. Eventually, we made it to California and I shelled out my own money for a ticket home on a commercial flight. Getting to Grand Butte involved a couple lay-overs and finally a puddle-jumper that put me down at the nearest airstrip, still fifty miles from home. I stood beside the road in my uniform and stuck out my thumb.

One thing I've learned in my years in the service is that people love soldiers. I don't know if it's a guilt thing or genuine gratitude, but I was constantly stopped by people who wanted to shake my hand and thank me for my service. Drivers apparently felt the same way, because I had no trouble getting rides. I arrived in Grand Butte at midnight, delivered right to my door.

There were no lights on in the house, but the dogs set up a racket. I guess they'd forgotten me. Old Blue would have remembered and made the rest of them shut up, but as it was, the noise roused my dad from his bed. He met me at the door cradling a double-barreled shotgun.

"It's me, Dad. Billy," I said hastily. It would be a shame to survive three tours in a war zone only to be plugged by my own father.

"Billy? What the hell? Quiet down, you dogs!"

Mom came running, tying the sash of her robe. "Billy? Is that you, son? Oh, Billy, come on in here and let me see you!"

So then all the lights were on in the house, the dogs were shushed, coffee was perking and Mom was at the stove frying eggs and ham on the grounds that I had to be hungry. They were so glad to see me, I put aside my anger for a while and just let myself feel happy to be home. When I couldn't keep my eyes open any longer, Mom made me a bed on the couch, because apparently my old room was now her sewing room, and I slept.

Morning brought back the memory of why I'd made this trip and with it, the anger. It was Saturday, so Dad didn't have to go to work. He was sitting on the front porch, smoking. I joined him, coffee cup in hand, hitching up one hip to sit on the railing so I could face him.

"Why didn't you tell me about Bree, Dad?" I asked.

"I guess your mother wrote to you," he said. "I told her not to. Damn fool woman. Women always think they gotta do something."

"Why didn't you tell me?" I persisted.

"Well, because you were gone and couldn't come home. Army's tough enough without being worried with something like that. We weren't sure if it was your kid, anyway. Bree was...."

"Don't say a word against her," I warned.

"Anyway, not much doubt about it now. Little girl looks just like you. I see 'em sometimes around town. Bree never speaks."

"Why should she? The whole family abandoned her," I said. "I'm going over there now."

"Maybe you'd better call first," Dad said, but I didn't bother to answer. It was time to go see my girls.

Mrs. Carrolton opened the door to my knock. Her face

reflected the shock she felt at the sight of me. "Bree's not home," she said before I could speak. "You go on now, you're not welcome here," she added, as if I was a stray dog that had wandered up to her doorstep.

"Mrs. Carrolton, I have a right to see my daughter," I said.

"Bree's not here," she repeated in a panicky voice. "Hank! Come here quick!"

Bree's father arrived at the door. He sized up the situation in one glance and stepped slightly in front of his wife, like he was protecting her.

"Hello, Billy," he said. "Of course, you have a right to see Bree and Emmy. They aren't home right now, but I'll tell her you were here asking for her. Are you staying with your folks?"

"Yes, sir," I said. "Where could I find Bree?"

"Well, Billy, I'd rather she have a little time to know you're home. Might be a pretty big shock for her if you just suddenly came up on her. I'll tell her to get in touch with you at your folks' house, okay?"

"It'll have to be, I guess," I said. "But tell her I really want to see her and Emmy."

There was nothing to do but leave. Mrs. Carrolton's white face stayed in my mind. Was she actually afraid of me? What had I done to inspire such fear in Bree's mother? Then it hit me: she was afraid I'd claim Emmy.

Emmy and I went to Uncle Charles' house early that day. John'd called and said Charles was asking for Emmy. He'd been going through some of the old stuff in the attic as part of his therapy to try to revive memories and found a cache of his childhood toys. He couldn't wait to show Emmy the rocking horse and big stuffed rabbit. So after breakfast, I packed up Emmy and off we went.

Emmy was delighted with Uncle Charles' stash. John carried everything out onto the lawn because the more time Charles spent outdoors, the better. Emmy yelled, "Horsy!" climbed right up on the horse although it was too big for her, and rocked furiously. Charles' smile as he watched her was pure joy. She insisted the big rabbit's name was Honey Bunny Too, just like her much smaller stuffed toy at home. There was a little china tea set and Charles and Emmy set the table and put Honey Bunny Too in a chair to have sips of air-tea with them. They were so engrossed in their make-believe world that John and I stood back and let them have at it.

"This is better for Charles than any medicine," John said. "He's more responsive with Emmy than with me or any of the therapists."

"Maybe he can relax because she accepts him just as he is," I said. "She doesn't judge."

John nodded. "Yeah. Must be nice."

"Do you feel judged?" I asked.

"Not by you. Not by anyone in Grand Butte, because they don't know about my past. That's why I love it here, I guess. Being liked, feeling welcomed and respected – well, I know it won't last, but it's been great."

"Why couldn't it last?"

"Once they know – and sooner or later, they will – everyone will be afraid and disgusted."

"What if people understood? What if the man you've become carried more weight than the kid you used to be?"

"You said it yourself: people won't stop for explanations when they hear the word pedophile," John said.

"But you're not that! You didn't know Sue was underage. It

seems so unfair that you're branded with that awful label when you don't deserve it."

"Being an ex-con is a pretty big deal, too," John said. "The best thing for me to do would be just to go now, before the news catches up with me. But Charles…."

He looked so sad, so dejected, that I impulsively hugged him. He returned the hug fervently. When I looked at him in surprise, he tipped up my face and kissed me.

"I'm sorry. I'm sorry," he stammered, letting me go immediately. "I got carried away. It won't happen again."

"You're damn right it won't, jerkface."

John was spun around by a powerful hand on his shoulder. The owner's other hand delivered a cracking punch to his jaw. He crumpled.

Billy was home.

~*~

Man, I saw red when that SOB kissed Bree. I had a hunch Bree might be visiting good ol' Uncle Charles, so I went there after I left her parents'. I was just rounding the corner of the house when I came upon them. Old Man Jacoby and a little girl – my little girl, Emmy, I guess – were having some kind of tea party, and right there in plain sight was Bree, kissing some strange guy. I didn't stop to think, I just punched him. Then Emmy started screaming and the old man got all agitated, waving his arms and hollering, and Bree was trying to help the strange guy up, and some damn little yapping dog was snapping at my leg. It was chaos.

Bree didn't have time to send me any more than a harried glance as she tried to get everybody settled down. The strange guy got to his feet and Emmy ran to him and hugged his knees, babbling "A'wight, John? A'wight?" Bree sat Mr.

Jacoby down and leaned over to talk right in his face, reassuring him that it was okay, he was okay, John was okay, and I was okay. Then she grabbed the little dog and got it to shut up. Finally, some kind of order was restored, and only then did she turn to me.

"Well, Billy," she said, "you haven't forgotten how to make an entrance."

"Aren't you glad to see me, Bree?" I asked. This wasn't the welcome I'd expected.

"I'd have been glad to see you a couple of years ago. Now I'm not so sure."

"So who's this Bozo?" I said, jerking my thumb in the stranger's direction.

"This is John Carver, Uncle Charles' caretaker. The man you just punched is the same one who saved my life, and Emmy's life, so thanks a lot, Billy," Bree said.

"I don't know anything about that," I said.

"He found our car after I'd wrecked on the road to town. If he hadn't pulled us out, we could well have gone over the cliff with the car. I owe him my life and Emmy's. It might be a good plan to have some idea what you're doing before you do it."

"Yeah, great and all that, but why are you kissing him?"

Bree gave me a "none of your business" look.

John Carver's head swiveled back and forth like he was watching a tennis match. Emmy had climbed him like a tree, and he was holding her against his shoulder and patting her back. It made my blood boil.

"Hey, dip-wad," I said. "Let me see my daughter."

But Emmy buried her face in his neck and wouldn't look at me. Bree took her gently and spoke quietly in her ear. Emmy shook her head and wouldn't look up. I could see her lower lip stuck out like a shelf.

"You don't want to encourage that kind of pouting, Bree," I said. "I've come halfway around the world to see this kid. Put her down and quit babying her."

Bree's eyes blazed but she kept her voice level. "Billy, you've caused enough trouble here for one day. You go on home, or wherever you're staying, and I'll see you later. In the meantime, don't you dare tell me how to take care of my daughter."

"My daughter, too," I reminded her.

"Only biologically. You have no other claim."

"I didn't even know she existed until Mom wrote to me last week."

"You knew where I was," Bree said.

"Okay, but—"

"You've been out of touch."

"But I'm here now."

She just looked at me. She didn't look happy.

~*~

So much for love's young dream. My jaw ached from the punch I'd just taken and I spit blood from where I'd bitten my tongue. And what had I done? Taken it, that's what, with not a single instinct to fight back. My gut feeling was that I deserved it.

Emmy was scared and wanted to be held. I picked her up automatically, soothing her as I'd done many times. She hid her face in my shoulder, whimpering and holding on tight with her arms and legs. Bree took her when Billy demanded to see her, but she wouldn't look at her daddy. She said, "John gots a boo-boo." Not a comment her father found endearing.

Charles was struggling to get out of the deep Adirondack chair. I went over and helped him to his feet. He leaned heavily on my arm as we went into the house. I'd let Bree deal with her little family in privacy. Charles didn't need any more excitement, anyway. We went into his study and I got him settled in his recliner with a blanket over his knees. I held the water glass up so he could sip through the straw. That was a skill he'd just relearned. He held up a finger, his signal he wanted to say something.

Charles' speech was still slurred. He'd become a man of few words, skipping adjectives and adverbs. I could understand everything he said because I heard it all the time, but right now he was upset and his language skills deteriorated commensurately.

"Bree a'right? You a'right?" he asked, his eyes fixed anxiously on mine.

"Bree's okay," I assured him. "Me, too. That guy out there, that's apparently Emmy's father."

"I nah," Charles said. "Bi-ye. Nah him long time. Ba' kid."

"Well, Bree will have to work that out for herself," I said.

"You kiss her," Charles said.

"Yeah. Guess I shouldn't have done that."

"Love her?" Charles asked, getting directly to the point.

"I do," I said. "But I don't have anything to offer her."

"Fi' for her," Charles said.

"I don't think..."

"Fi' for her!" he repeated emphatically.

Then he closed his eyes, signaling the conversation was over.

I looked out the window to check on Bree and Emmy and saw they were alone in the back yard. But somehow, I didn't want to join them just then. The memory of my passivity in the face of Billy's attack burned me with shame. I figured she must think I was the world's biggest wuss. Even Charles thought so. I scribbled a note to tell him I'd be out for a few minutes, put it on his lap where he'd be sure to see it, and headed out the front door. I'd try to walk off my feelings since there was no place else to put them.

The land around Charles' house was virgin woods, with big, old-growth timber. Coyotes lived there, and foxes. I'd hear them yipping sometimes at night. There was a stream, and once I spotted tracks, evidence a bear had been fishing there. I kept a wary eye peeled when I was deep in the forest, and was careful to make a lot of noise as I hiked. The animals, like everyone else, were happy to steer clear of me if they had enough warning.

Usually the forest was a balm for whatever troubled me, but today my mind churned. I wanted to find Billy and pound him. I wanted to go to Bree and beg her to love me. I wanted to run as far and as fast as I could from this place and all its complications. In my agitation, I walked farther than I ever had, and when I paused to catch my breath I realized nothing looked familiar. Don't panic, I told myself. All you have to do is follow the stream. But follow it in which direction? It meandered all over the place. The sun was directly overhead, so it was no help in determining east or west. I sat down and leaned against a tree trunk. Screw it, I thought. So I'm lost. So I never go back. Who's going to care?

Well, Charles would. I was important to him because he needed me, but what was I to him, really? Paid help. Replaceable. Nobody else would even notice I was gone. Maybe Emmy might ask for me a time or two, but she'd soon forget. Bree would be back with Billy, happy with her child's father.

In the depth of my self-pity, I heard something approaching through the dried leaves that carpeted the forest floor. I scrambled to my feet, envisioning an enraged mama bear, ready to tear me apart. Or it could be a rabid coyote. Or…

It was Queenie. She'd apparently followed me from the house, gotten side-tracked by some interesting scent and was just now catching up. I bent down to pet her and she stuck her cold nose in my face and licked my bruised jaw. I had to laugh. Big threat, Queenie was. And yet, when I didn't know what was coming, my body had been suffused with adrenalin and I was ready to fight or flee. Perception is everything.

What if the things I feared were my perceptions, not reality? I remembered when I was a kid, having a run-in with my friends on the playground. Even then, I was miserably concerned with whether they still liked me, what they thought of me. My mother said they probably weren't thinking of me at all because most people are usually thinking about themselves.

But the reality of my situation as an ex-con and convicted pedophile was bad enough to capture the attention of anyone who heard about it. And I thought I knew what would follow: contempt, shunning, isolation, maybe more pokes on the jaw. It would break my heart to leave Grand Butte, but it would be best to get away before I was run out of town.

Queenie regarded me with her head on one side. She ran a few feet, then ran back to me. Clearly, she didn't think this was the time or place for introspection.

"All right, girl, I said, "take me home. I mean, back. Take me back."

~*~

After I'd convinced Billy to leave, I carried Emmy into the

house and went to check on Uncle Charles in his recliner. He waved a scrap of paper at me.

"John gah," he said.

"What? Gone where?" I said.

"Walk," Charles said.

"Oh," I said, relieved. I'd thought there was a good possibility that John would simply take off after Billy's attack. I realized how much I didn't want that to happen.

Charles held up one finger. "Ca' George, I wan' talk t' him."

George McMasters was Charles long-time lawyer and friend. I thought it was a good thing he wanted to see one of his friends again. They'd come calling, that loyal band of quasi-brothers who'd been buddies since they were toddlers, but Charles had sent them away.

"Don' wan' 'em see me," he'd said.

But now he was asking for George. I stifled thoughts that it wasn't a good day for a visit, went to the phone, dialed and handed the phone to Charles.

"You come?" Charles said into the phone.

Of course, George was delighted. He said yes, he'd be there in half an hour and he'd bring lunch, their favorite cheeseburgers from the diner. Charles looked livelier than I'd seen him as he told me this. He indicated he wanted the little table in his study set, and asked the housekeeper to make a fresh pot of decaf.

When George arrived, I ushered him into the study and left the two men alone. I needed to go home. Emmy was hungry; it was 'way past her lunch time. She was exhausted from the emotionally-fraught morning we'd just had, and was working toward a major melt-down. As I buckled her into her car seat, I saw John and Queenie emerging from the woods. I waved, but Emmy's wails were explanation enough for why I couldn't stay. I was glad for the excuse; I didn't want to talk to John yet. What had happened with Billy was just too embarrassing. I needed time to collect myself.

Later, Emmy having been fed and put down for a nap she was too tired to refuse, I sat outside on the patio and allowed myself to replay earlier events. Billy was home. He wanted to see Emmy. He seemed to want me again. He was different – strong, tough, decisive – not the too-cool-for-school Billy who'd left me. I hated that he'd punched John, but there was something exciting and flattering about his instant action. He'd been jealous when he saw John kissing me. That meant he still cared, didn't it? But how dared he tell me how to handle Emmy? He didn't know her, didn't know me anymore, for that matter. That bossiness was the other side of the new assertive Billy, and it was a side I didn't like.

John. Aside from the eternal debt of gratitude I owed him for saving me and Emmy, I'd grown to like him. A lot. He'd trusted me enough to reveal his secret, and it was a big one. I thought I understood his need to keep moving and his wistful wish to stay. I'd felt it myself. As for his status as a so-called pedophile, it was ridiculous. He'd only been a horny teenager who'd gotten in over his head. If anybody could relate, it'd be me. Yet he was right when he said some people wouldn't wait around to hear the extenuating circumstances. Two powerful words, pedophilia and prison, would be all they'd need to hear.

Whatever dawning feelings I had for John were swamped now by Billy's return. What did I want from him? Did I want him to take his place as Emmy's father, with all the rights and privileges that entailed? But she was my baby. His parenthood was simply biological; I'd done all the heavy lifting. Who did he think he was, to swoop in and take over? Yet...he was Billy. My first love. Emmy deserved a daddy.

Could we possibly become a family, after the misunderstandings and missed connections? Did I even still want that?

All these questions demanded answers and there was only one way to get them. I had to talk to Billy.

# Chapter Six

Emmy was a cute little thing, but I could see Bree was letting her become a brat. Both of them needed a firm hand, some discipline and structure. I'd been absent from their lives, but now I was back and ready to lead. Bree resented it right now, but she'd get over it. That's something I learned in the Army: there's a lot of safety and security in the chain of command once you surrender your will to it.

Bree insisted I leave her uncle's place, so I went on back to my folks'. They were having lunch and Mom immediately jumped up from the table to fix me a plate. I sat down and ate with them, and after the meal we had coffee and I told them Army stories. Mom looked worried, but Dad loved it – all the blood and guts and camaraderie appealed to him in a very basic way. I could see a new look in his eyes when he glanced at me, something I'd never seen before. Respect.

"Looks like you've become a man, son," he said. "What do you think you'll want to do when your time is up?"

"Reenlist," I said. "The Army's my career. I've already made rank as an NCO and I intend to keep moving up. It's hard to become an officer without a college degree, so I'm taking online courses. Once I have the diploma, I'll apply to Officer's Candidate School and I'm confident I'll be accepted. Army life as an officer is pretty darn sweet, and I'll be able to retire in my fifties with some great bennies."

"Sounds like you've thought it through," Dad said. "What about your – What about Bree and the baby?"

"That's what I came home to see about. I have a duty to support my child, so if Bree wants to get married, she and Emmy can come with me after this tour is over. It'll mean a lot of moving from base to base, but Army wives are a close-knit bunch. She'll get used to it. It'd be a black mark against me if it became known I had an illegitimate child, so it would actually be better for me to marry Bree. Having a presentable family is good for an officer. There are lots of social duties for a wife."

Mom frowned. "But do you want to be married to Bree?" she asked timidly. "It doesn't seem like a reason to get married, just because you need a hostess. And wouldn't it be a pretty hard life for kids? Emmy would have to go to a lot of different schools. She'd never know where she belonged."

"Yeah, well, that teaches a kid to be resourceful," I said. Discussion closed. No point in talking about my plans to people who didn't get it, even if one of them was my mother. What did she know about Army life? She'd lived her entire existence in the same little dot on the map, but I was done with small towns. It's a big world out there and I intended to see more of it.

I headed back over to Bree's parents' house, hoping to catch her home and alone. Luck was with me. She was sitting by herself on the patio, staring out over the green lawn. She didn't hear me coming and jumped when I said her name.

"Oh, Billy," she said. "I was just thinking that I need to talk to you."

"So talk, babe," I said. "Here I am."

"Why did you come home now, after all this time?"

"I just found out you'd had a baby when Mom wrote to me a week ago," I said. "I got home as fast as I could."

"But you just went off and left me," Bree said quietly. "I was pregnant and when I went to your house to tell you, I had to find out from your dad that you were gone. You couldn't even tell me yourself; you didn't even say goodbye. Then you didn't call or write or come home. I had to figure things out alone. Now all of a sudden, you're back. What do you want, Billy?"

"Look, I didn't handle things very well," I said. "Daw was talking about putting me in jail if I didn't get the hell out of town and stay out. I admit it was chicken-shit of me not to tell you about it myself. Then when I got into the Army, it just, I don't know, it just filled me up so I didn't have room for anything else in my mind. And I didn't know you were pregnant. Just awful timing, I guess."

"That's for sure," Bree said. "And yet, I got Emmy out of it, and I love her more than anything in the world."

"I'm willing to do the right thing by you, Bree," I said. "If you want to get married, we will. You and Emmy can stay here until my tour in Afghanistan is over. Then when I know where I'll be based, I'll send for you."

"That sounds more like a business proposal than a marriage proposal," Bree said. "I didn't hear the word 'love' mentioned."

In answer, I pulled her up from her chair, took her in my arms and kissed her. It was her second kiss of the day. She didn't respond at first, but then her arms went around my neck and she kissed me back. I felt a familiar tug of excitement and I think she did, too. We were back in high school again, Bree 'n Billy, free and wild and ready for whatever life had in store.

Our kiss was ended by Emmy's voice: "Mama! Up!"

"Oops," Bree said, "guess who's awake."

That was that. Bree brought Emmy outside, but when she saw me she stuck out her lip and refused to come to me. "John gots boo-boo," she said, looking up at her mother with big eyes. So Bree set Emmy on her grandpa's immaculate grass and let her play. We watched her, Bree's face reflecting all the love and pride she felt for her little girl. Emmy was cute, and she sure did look like me, I had to admit. I was annoyed that she hadn't taken to me, though. The kid needed a firm father's hand, even if she didn't think she liked me right now. Good thing I was back in the picture.

Kissing Billy was almost like old times. But something was missing and I couldn't put my finger on exactly what it was. Maybe I reacted differently because I was a mother now, not a teenage girl. Or maybe we'd been apart too long. I kissed him back, but it just wasn't working for me. Then Emmy called me and I was relieved to have an excuse to step away.

She still didn't like him. Emmy could remember at least for a while things that made a big impression on her. Seeing Billy hit John and John's bloody face had definitely made an impression. She told me over and over about John's boo-boo. I think she was worried about him, as much as a two-year-old can worry. In any case, she remembered she didn't like Billy.

And he wasn't good with her. He seemed to think he could just step into the parental role without even getting to know her. In his mind, fathers issued orders and children and wives obeyed. I didn't agree with his instant assessment that Emmy was spoiled. She responded just fine to people who loved her.

It seemed, with the innate sense of dogs and children, she'd decided this guy didn't love her.

And that made me not love him.

When I entered the house, I saw the door to the study was closed, which was unusual. I listened for a minute and heard Charles' garbled speech and another low voice. He had company; I nodded in approval. He'd been avoiding his friends, and friends meant a lot to Charles. I was glad he was reconnecting.

Queenie followed me upstairs to my room and we both stretched out on the bed. Naps were not part of my daily routine, but Charles seemed to be occupied and I was beat. Beat up, as well. My jaw ached, my head ached and my feet ached from my hike. Feeling as old as Charles and almost as feeble, I closed my eyes. Queenie curled cozily beside me and we slept.

I awoke disoriented, feeling like it was morning, but a glance at the bedside clock told me only an hour had passed. I'd slept hard and felt better. It was the housekeeper's afternoon off, so Charles would be on his own in the study. I normally checked on him every few minutes. I jumped to my feet and ran down the stairs. The study door was slightly ajar but there were no voices from within, so Charles' guest must have gone.

I tapped lightly on the open door and went in. He was in his recliner with his head at a strange angle. He's going to have a stiff neck when he wakes up, I thought. I said his name, but he was really out of it, so I touched his shoulder. I knew then. I reached for my phone.

Dr. Martin came, and Daw, but there was nothing to do but call the mortuary. Dr. Martin said that because it was an unexpected home death, there would be an autopsy. Daw asked where I'd been that afternoon. I was ashamed to say I'd been sleeping, but I told the truth. I saw the brief look the men exchanged.

Bree and her mother arrived then, and Mrs. Carrolton immediately burst into tears. She kept saying, "He was my last remaining relative. Now my whole birth family is gone." Bree knelt by Charles' side and stroked his face. She picked up his furrowed old hand and kissed it, then put it carefully back in his lap. Her eyes shone with unshed tears, but she didn't cry.

"He's been struggling," she said quietly to her mother. "I'm glad he doesn't have to struggle any longer."

I silently agreed, but my guilt rendered me mute. I didn't have the right to mourn this man who'd been so good to me. Maybe if I'd been doing what I got paid to do, he'd still be alive. I was thinking I'd better go upstairs and pack when Daw spoke.

"I'm going to have to ask you to stay put, John," he said. "Just until after the autopsy gives us the cause of death. Charles was old and sick, and while we didn't expect him to die right now, it's not much of a stretch to think his time had come. But we have to know for sure."

So once again, the local lawman told me not to leave town. I was stuck to Grand Butte like gum on the sole of a shoe.

"Should I stay here in the house?" I asked.

"Don't see why not," Daw said. "You've been living here, no reason to move right now. Doc will do the autopsy himself, probably tomorrow. Kathleen will want to have the funeral as soon as possible."

~*~

Every person in town except the totally bed-ridden came to Charles' funeral. The church was a garden of flowers, their fragrance heavy in the air. The service was traditional – a eulogy, a short sermon, congregational singing and a heart-rending rendition of Ave Maria by a boys' choir. I stood in the back near the door, listening to the boys' pure voices soaring up to heaven, feeling the prick of tears behind my eyes. Bree was far away with her family in the front pew.

I didn't go to the burial. Seeing Charles lowered into the earth was something I didn't want etched in my memory. Mrs. Carrolton had planned a reception at Charles' house afterward, so I went back to see what I could do to help. I was still setting up folding chairs when the first cars crunched up the gravel drive. It seemed the whole town had come back to the house. I saw Patsy from the diner, Daw and Janie, Dr. Martin, Charles' band of buddies, Mrs. Willett and lots of people I knew only by sight – but I didn't see Billy.

Bree was fully occupied with receiving condolences and making sure everyone had a plate and a full glass, so I didn't have a chance to speak to her until almost everyone had left. There were dark purple circles under her eyes, the scar on her forehead was an angry pink and she was limping. She looked exhausted and sad and beautiful.

"I'm so sorry for your loss," I said. "I'll miss him, too."

"I know you will, John," she said, taking my hand. "You were his life support system these last few weeks."

"Apparently not a very good one," I said.

"You are not allowed to blame yourself because he died while you were taking a nap," she said firmly. "If we want to cast blame, what about the scene I brought down on him in his own backyard? Billy's theatrics couldn't have been good for Charles. I know he was upset."

"You don't get to blame yourself, either," I said. "You aren't responsible for somebody else's behavior. Besides, Charles felt well enough to get together with one of his friends that same day. It was the first time he'd reached out to any of his pals."

"It was George McMasters who came to visit. Charles asked me to call him and George came right away. Charles must have died soon after he left. The autopsy results should be available by the end of the week," Bree said. "But I feel sure I know the cause of death. I think he had another stroke right there in his recliner."

"That's what I think, too. Charles was frail and his recovery was never a sure thing. I guess if he had to go, it would have been the way he wanted it – peacefully, at home. That's the way any of us would want it."

"I'm grateful he never had to go back to the rehab place, or worse yet, to a nursing home. He'd have hated it. You saved him from that, John."

Just then, Bree's mother motioned her over to say goodbye to an elderly couple who were heading toward the door. I never got a chance to ask her where Billy was, or who was watching Emmy. Guess it really wasn't my business anyway.

I told Bree I wouldn't go to the funeral. Old Man Jacoby never liked me and the feeling was mutual. No way was I going to be a hypocrite and pretend I was sad. I offered to watch Emmy, but Bree said she'd already arranged for a baby-sitter. Just as well. Emmy still didn't like me, although I was confident I could win her over if I took the time. She was just a baby, after all.

I felt twitchy and restless. The town was stifling me like it did when I was a teenager. One night I dreamed of Phu Quoc, a Vietnamese island where I'd gone on my last leave. Ong Lang Beach was paradise. I stayed in a little hotel right on the sand, with a gorgeous Vietnamese girl for company. She was expensive, but worth every penny.

When I woke, I felt homesick for a place on the other side of the world that had never been my home. I knew I couldn't stick around Grand Butte much longer, although I was far from sure about Bree. Her feelings for me seemed to have changed, and to be honest, I didn't have the same feelings for her, either. The two kids we used to be were gone, but they'd created a new human before they left. I felt bad about that.

Well, I'd made Bree the offer, and if she wanted marriage, I'd honor that offer. I felt like it was the least I could do. But meanwhile, I had to get going.

It was time to go back to work at the bank full-time. My injuries had almost healed and there were no more excuses. Reluctantly, I surrendered Emmy to my folks and trooped off to work the Monday after Charles' funeral. Everyone was very nice and helpful – it was Grand Butte, after all – but it was a long, long day. Standing on my feet at the teller window reminded me forcefully of those newly-healed bones in my foot, and perching on the high stool someone thoughtfully provided made my ribs ache. Then at the end of the day, my cash drawer wouldn't balance and I had to stay until I found the error. It was almost six o'clock when I limped in the door of my parents' house. Emmy met me with a crashing hug around the knees that almost knocked me down. My father looked almost as worn out as I did.

"If God meant for old men to look after two-year-olds, he would have reversed the aging process," he grumbled.

"Daddy, I'm sorry," I said, tears of exhaustion springing to my eyes. "I know it's hard to watch her all day and I'm so grateful to you."

"Oh, for heaven's sake, you two!" my mother said. "Just listen to the pair of you, boo-hoo, such a sad life. Come on, let's eat some dinner and see if you can catch your second wind."

Mom couldn't empathize with weariness because she was a perpetual ball of energy. I wished she'd stay home more and spend some of that energy helping with Emmy, but I was in no position to dictate terms. I was darn lucky to have their help.

"Billy came around today," Dad said as we cleared the table. "I had a hard time convincing him not to go to the bank to see you."

"Oh, that would have been all I needed," I said.

"Just what do you need, Bree?" Dad asked gently. "What are your intentions with that young man? He isn't a boy anymore and he's not going to hang around very long waiting for you. He told me he's ready to go back to Afghanistan."

"I don't know, I really don't know," I said. "He's been gone so long, and so much happened to me while he was away. To him, too, I guess. He's different now. I feel like we're not the same people we were."

"You're not," Dad said. "You've both grown up fast in the past couple of years. Play time is over. The decision you make now will affect the rest of your lives. Think about it very carefully."

"Well, I don't think he's the one for you," Mom said with her usual decisiveness. "Has he even proposed?"

"He said we could get married if I wanted to," I said.

"Hmmph. Not very romantic," she said.

"No, but he is Emmy's father. Maybe I owe it to her to let her grow up with her daddy."

"In a perfect world, I'd say yes to that," Dad said. "I'm all for dads. But think about it, Bree. Do you want to move from

Army base to base, maybe some of them overseas, with a toddler? Are your feelings for Billy strong enough to sustain you when you're away from everything you know and love? Will he support you emotionally as well as financially?"

"Right now the only support I want is my bed," I said, short-circuiting the discussion I was just too tired to continue.

But I wouldn't be resting, not any time soon. As soon as I got Emmy settled for the night, Billy knocked on the door.

"We have to talk," he said.

"Isn't that supposed to be the girl's line?" I said.

But he didn't laugh. "Come on. Let's go for a drive."

What Billy wanted to tell me was that he was leaving the next day. He said he couldn't stand sticking around this town and was cutting his leave short.

"That must be a first for the Army," I said.

"You'd be surprised," Billy said. "Quite a few guys come back early. It's tough to go between home and the battlefield. Sometimes it's just easier to keep your focus on the area where you might get killed and not allow yourself to be distracted by home. The point is, Bree, I need to know where I stand with you before I go."

"I don't know," I said. "I need more time."

"We're out of time," Billy said.

"By your choice," I reminded him.

"Look, I'll keep in touch this time. You think about it. If you decide you want to get married, let me know. But if you don't, let me know that, too. Don't leave me hanging with no word."

He heard what he'd just said and actually blushed. As well he should. We parted with a chaste kiss. I was relieved to see him go.

~*~

Daw came out to tell me the results of the autopsy. The report said Charles Jacoby died of natural causes: he'd suffered a catastrophic stroke. I felt a little better knowing that even if I'd been sitting in the same room, Charles couldn't have survived. Still, he died alone while I was snoozing and I hated that. Daw said I was free to leave now if that's what I wanted to do.

"I don't have any choice," I said. "I've got no job and no place to live. It's time for me to be moving on."

"John, if you want to stay you can come and live with Janie and me until you get settled. We'd be glad to have you. There aren't a whole lot of jobs in this small town, but if you're willing to drive twenty miles to the city, I bet you could find something there. The commute's not so bad, except in the winter."

"Thanks, but I couldn't take advantage of you and Janie like that. I love Grand Butte, and you've all been great, but there's no future for me here."

"What about Bree?" Daw asked.

"What do you mean?" I couldn't meet his eye.

"Son, anybody with one eye can see how you feel about her," Daw said. "Janie noticed it the first time she saw you together."

"I've got nothing to offer her," I said. "No job, no home, no prospects."

"Look, you're a healthy young man," Daw said, exasperation tingeing his voice. "Maybe you need to settle down, stop drifting and take hold of your life, grow some roots."

I was briefly thankful he didn't say I needed to grow some balls. I knew I needed to do that, too. "Bree doesn't feel the same way about me. I'm not a very good catch. Besides, Billy's home now and she'll choose him."

"I heard Billy's gone back to his base. Why don't you stick around and let Bree decide what she wants," Daw said.

He was kind, Daw was, but he didn't know how bad a catch I actually was. I marveled anew that he'd never run my name through his criminal data base. You'd think simple curiosity about a stranger in town would have warranted that much detective work. And had he known, there'd have been no offers of guest rooms. Nope, it's always good to leave before you're tossed out. I shook Daw's hand, thanked him again for his kindness and said I'd be leaving tomorrow. Then I called Mrs. Carrolton and arranged to drop Queenie off on my way out of town. I'd grown fond of that little brown dog, but she wasn't mine. None of this was mine.

Early the next morning, the phone rang. I didn't have an extension in my bedroom, and the house was empty except for me. I groped my way downstairs to Charles' study and picked up the desk phone. It was Charles' friend and lawyer, George McMasters.

"Sorry to call so early," he said, "but Daw said you're planning to leave town today. Before you go, it's very important that you come by my office. Charles left you something in his will."

That was totally unexpected. I liked Charles and felt he liked me, but I was his paid helper. I never expected he'd leave me anything. Well, I never expected he'd die on me, for that matter.

"Of course," I said to Mr. McMasters. "What time shall I be there?"

"Make it 10 AM."

When I entered the lawyer's reception room, I was surprised to see Bree there, too. "What's up?" I asked her.

"No idea," she replied. "George just said to come at ten. I had to ask for time off work, which didn't go over well. Hope this doesn't take long."

We were ushered into Mr. McMasters' office and seated in front of his desk. After the good mornings were exchanged, he smoothed out the document that lay on the blotter before him and began to read Charles' will. He'd been a wealthy man, more than I'd suspected. There were bequests to the housekeeper and groundskeeper and other people who'd worked for him over the years, and to a number of charities. The rest of his cash went to Bree's mother, his only surviving relative. Then Mr. McMasters got to the reason we'd been summoned.

Charles left his house to us. To Bree and me jointly, with the proviso that the house be occupied by one or both of us for one year before it could be sold. A fund was provided for its upkeep. Whoever didn't live in the house was required to stay in Grand Butte during that year. If the conditions of the will were met when time was up, we were free to sell it and split the money. Mr. McMasters folded his hands and looked at us.

My mouth was hanging open, and so was Bree's. "What? He did what?" she sputtered.

"He left his house to you and John," Mr. McMasters repeated patiently. "One or both of you must live in the house for a year before you can put it on the market. There's a fund to pay for utilities and upkeep. If you don't fulfill the terms of the will, the house will be sold by the executor of the estate (that's me, by the way), and the proceeds will go to charity. I guess this is a shock."

That was a nice bit of understatement. What the hell was I going to do with half a great, big house? Why had Charles done such a crazy thing? Bree and I weren't married, we weren't even a couple, and now we were anchored together for a year by a house. What was he thinking?

Mr. McMasters handed Bree a single sheet of paper. "He left you this letter," he said. "He wanted to revise his will on the day he died, that's why he called me. I don't know, maybe he had some kind of premonition of his death. After we finished the will and got the housekeeper and the groundskeeper to witness it, he asked me to stay while he wrote this letter. It took him an hour and he was exhausted when he finished, but I can testify that he was fully compos mentis. I took the liberty of having it typed since Charles' handwriting is difficult to read."

Bree read it aloud:

> Dearest Bree,
>
> By now George has told you that I have left you half my house and enough money to maintain it. That's so you'll always have a place to live, but also leaves you with an incentive to work. Knowing what to do with your life has been hard for you. I hope you will find what you love.
>
> By the end of the year, it will be clear to you why I left half the house to John. The passage of time can produce surprising results. John thinks his life is over, but it's only just begun.
>
> When the year is up, you are free to do as you choose with my old house. One of you may buy the other out, you may sell it and split the profits, turn it into a bed and breakfast, or - who knows? Whatever happens, I love you and want you and John to have the happy life you both deserve.
>
> Please take care of Queenie. She's a good dog.
>
> Your loving Uncle Charles

.

# Chapter Seven

Mr. McMasters acted like it was the most ordinary thing in the world for two unrelated young people to co-inherit a mansion. He said he'd get busy on the paperwork, ushered us to the door, shook our hands, and deposited us back on the sidewalk. We stood there looking at each other blankly. Then, without exchanging a word, we walked to the coffee shop and got ourselves a booth.

"I guess you might as well stay put," Bree said, "since you're already living there. I can't move in with Emmy, I need my folks to watch her while I'm at work."

"What am I going to do all day long without Charles to take care of?" I said. "I mean, I can cut the grass and, I don't know, repair things. It's a big place, it'll take a lot of maintenance. But still…"

"If you could just give it a month," Bree said, "to let us get our heads around this and figure out what to do."

"There's nothing to stop me from saying thanks, but no

thanks, leaving town this afternoon and just letting you have it all," I said, "and that's probably what I should do."

"But remember, if one of us walks away, neither of us gets anything. I don't know about you, but I could use the money." Bree said. "The house is worth a fortune; I don't know exactly how much, but we can find out. At the end of a year, we'll sell it and you'll get your half."

"Is there a market in this little town for such a grand house? Can anybody here afford it?" I asked.

"We're not quite that small a pond. There are a few big fish and one of them will want the house, I'm sure of it. Charles was right to specify occupancy – an empty house gets into all kinds of trouble. But it's not fair for all the upkeep to fall on you."

"Look, we need time for all this to settle," I said. "Like you said, let's take a month. Does anybody else know about the will?"

"My folks know, I guess, since Mom gets most of Charles' money. Probably nobody else knows, at least not yet."

"Then let's keep it to ourselves. If anybody wonders why I'm still there, we'll say I'm a temporary caretaker while the estate is being settled."

That's how we left it. I continued to live in the house, and I was right about the long days. Since the housekeeper and the lawn guy were both dismissed with the legacies Charles left them, it was just me. I puttered around outside, cutting grass, trimming, washing down the patio furniture. Then I explored the house. I'd never been all through it, but now I opened every door. It was even larger than I'd thought. There were six bedrooms furnished with heavy, old-fashioned beds and bureaus, each with its own bathroom. Windows were swathed with cloudy sheer curtains and musty velvet draperies. I left footprints in the dust of the carpets. Charles hadn't asked his housekeeper to clean the whole house; she'd confined her activities to the kitchen, our bedrooms and the living area.

One rainy Monday when I couldn't work outside, I found the vacuum cleaner, got a rag and a bucket of soapy water and cleaned one of the bedrooms. I took the curtains to the dry cleaner, washed the windows, scrubbed the bathroom and wiped down everything in sight. It looked and smelled so much better.

It kept raining, so I kept cleaning for the rest of the week. In the evenings, I looked at my prune-like hands and contemplated the strange curve ball life had thrown me.

My days fell into a kind of rhythm. There was a lot of work, almost too much for one person. But it was the kind of work that still gave me time to think. What would I do if my secret came out, now that I was tied to the town for an entire year? How did Bree really feel about Billy? When the year was up, would she take her money, marry him and move to some distant Army base? If she was no longer in Grand Butte, I knew the town would lose most of its allure for me. But where would I go next? Was there anywhere in the world where I could live peacefully without the fear of becoming an instant pariah if my past became known? And my past would inevitably become known since I'd have to register as a sex offender wherever I might try to settle. Those were the thoughts that kept me awake at night.

Bree was busy, too, working full-time at the bank and caring for Emmy at night. Our paths didn't often cross, but she did bring Emmy to the house on a bright Saturday morning. I'd just finished cutting the grass, and the place looked good. When Bree complimented me on it, I couldn't resist showing her the newly-cleaned bedrooms.

"Oh, wow!" she said. "I remember how neglected these rooms were. Charles closed them off years ago and lived downstairs. It seems a shame, all this wasted space, doesn't it?"

"Yeah, I rattle around in here," I said. "Are you sure you don't want to live in the house yourself, and I'll move out?"

"I wouldn't dream of asking you to move," Bree said, "but I do think about living here sometimes. There's no privacy at my folks' house and Dad is complaining more and more about watching Emmy. He hurt his back and lifting her is painful for him now."

"But if you moved in, it would cause a major scandal, right?" I said.

"Oh, probably, for a few days," she said, "but people here are like people anywhere – they're preoccupied with their own lives. My folks would have a fit initially, but I bet they'd be secretly relieved. I had to give up my apartment while I was recuperating from my injuries. Couldn't afford to pay the rent. So now they're stuck with me, and I'm pretty sure their plans for this stage in their lives didn't include a boomerang daughter and a lively toddler turning their home into a circus."

"Well, there's plenty of room here, that's for sure," I said, trying to keep my voice casual while my heart boomed with hope. "Charles' master suite has a little dressing room off of it that would be perfect for Emmy. You girls would have the downstairs to yourselves."

"There's still the day-care issue," Bree said. "I checked into the Methodist church's program. It's really good, but it would take almost my whole paycheck to put Emmy there."

"Maybe she wouldn't have to go every day," I said, thinking out loud. "Maybe you could split her time between day-care, your dad one day a week, and me a couple of days?"

"With you? Are you serious?"

"I don't blame you if you don't trust me with her," I said, feeling my face grow hot. What had I been thinking? No mother in her right mind would leave her little girl with a convicted pedophile.

"No, no, it's not that!" Bree said, looking horrified. "I didn't mean it that way at all. I just meant she's a handful right now, and you're not used to kids her age, and you've got this big house to keep."

"If there were two adults in the house, the work could be shared a bit. Of course, I know you're working full-time, so I'd still do most of it."

I could see the wheels turning in her head. "Well, it's something to think about," she said.

John's suggestion stuck in my mind. Life at Mom and Dad's was growing more fraught by the day. Dad had turned into a cranky old man since he'd hurt his back, and Emmy didn't understand that Papa couldn't give her piggy-back rides and throw her up to the sky any more. She got progressively whinier. Mom's solution to family angst was to stay gone most of the day. She'd volunteered at the new women's shelter and at the assisted living center. I'd have thought home preferable to either of those places, so it gave me an idea of how uncomfortable things really were.

The last straw came when Emmy ran away. She and Dad were out in the yard when she heard the ice-cream truck. She took off like a little deer, straight for the street, with Dad hobbling as fast as he could, which wasn't very fast, behind her. He yelled her name, told her to stop, but she paid no attention. Dad said he lost several years off of his life when she darted into the street in front of the truck. Luckily, the ice-cream man was paying attention and only going about ten miles per hour, so no harm was done. Except to my poor father, who was still white-faced and shaking when I got home from work.

He sat me down after Emmy was in bed and said, "Bree, it's not safe for me to look after Emmy. I can't move fast enough now to keep up with her. We could have lost her this afternoon. Your mother isn't interested in becoming a full-time baby-sitter, and she shouldn't have to be. I'll pay to enroll Emmy in a good day-care program."

"But Dad, do you know how much it costs? I've looked into it," I said, fighting tears. "You've been wonderful to Emmy, and you're right to know your limits now. Thank you so much for your generous offer, but Emmy is my responsibility. I'll think of something."

I went for a long walk and examined my options. I could quit my job and look after Emmy myself, but that meant more sponging off my parents. Although I didn't love my job, I sure didn't want to return to the total dependence of childhood. I could allow Mom and Dad to pay for my child's day-care, but I'd already taken enough from my parents. I had some pride left. I could marry Billy and move to an Army base somewhere. Emmy would have a father and we'd have a home. But I wasn't sure if I even still loved him. It just seemed too uncertain, too big a jump.

Then there was Charles' will. If John and I didn't fulfill its terms, there'd be no money, and I was already counting on it to jump-start my life. I thought long and hard about the last option: I could move into the house and take John up on his offer to look after Emmy part-time. None of these possibilities held much appeal, but I tried to evaluate each one rationally, without emotion.

Moving into Charles' house seemed to be my best bet. Somehow I had total faith in John's ability to care for Emmy, which was strange considering our relatively brief acquaintance and how protective I felt about my daughter.

He and Emmy got along well and he seemed to genuinely enjoy her company. The town would talk, for sure, but then they'd grow accustomed to our arrangement and move on.

Unless. Unless they heard about John's past. People who didn't know him would never understand how I could leave my baby with a so-called pervert. My parents, in particular, would both keel over and die on the spot. Yet, I believed my family, friends and neighbors would accept John if they knew the whole story.

Meanwhile, there was tomorrow. Dad was clearly at the end of his rope, but I couldn't just walk out on my co-workers with no notice. I pulled out my cell phone and called John. When I explained what had happened, I didn't have to say any more.

"Bring her here tomorrow," he said instantly. "She and I will spend the day together. It'll be a good trial run to see how it works out."

So I did.

~*~

I'd never been around kids for any length of time, but I liked them in theory. Emmy was bright and funny, but also firmly in the grip of what Bree called the Terrible Twos. Her favorite word was no, and she used it automatically, even to answer questions like, "How about some ice cream?" But she was no match for my wily use of psychology and it became a game to distract and disarm her before her stubbornness set in.

She was an affectionate little thing, and my heart melted when she put her arms around my neck and gave me a big, sloppy kiss that left my cheek dripping. That first day, I didn't have a plan. We went for a walk, brushed Queenie, played hide and seek, colored in her coloring book and hunted for pretty stones. When I looked at the clock, it was only 10 AM.

I briefly considered turning on the television, but I didn't know what kind of programs Emmy was allowed to watch and I didn't want to just plunk her down in front of the electronic baby-sitter. I dipped into the bag of toys and supplies Bree had brought and found a cache of books. We settled into a big chair and I read to her. Emmy said some of the words of the familiar stories along with me.

At lunch time, I carried her peanut butter and jelly sandwich, juice box and apple slices outside and we had a picnic. Bree'd said Emmy was giving up her naps, but I thought it was worth a try. After she'd eaten, I settled her on the couch, sat down beside her and told her a story. I'd never made up a story for a toddler before. Apparently it was boring, because Emmy's eyes drifted shut and she slept.

When Bree arrived after work, her little girl was rested, fed, clean and playing in the sunshine with Queenie. She thanked me with a hug, and I felt I'd been well-rewarded.

"Same time tomorrow?" I asked.

"Are you up for it?"

"Sure."

And so it began.

~*~

I couldn't stop thinking about Bree and Emmy after I got back to base. It wasn't good to be distracted in a war zone, and a couple of my buddies pointed that out to me several times. The last thing I needed was to be preoccupied with thoughts of a wife and baby; well, the next to last thing. The very last thing I needed was to get shot, or cause one of my men to get shot. I tried to focus.

At night when I lay in my bunk waiting for sleep, I'd see Emmy's little mini-me face, lower lip stuck out in a pout, turning away. I'd see Bree, the wild kid she used to be, the grown woman she was now. But I could never envision our future. Maybe it was too late for a future with her. I wondered how we'd gotten so far off-track.

I wasn't much of a letter writer, but I started letters to Bree half a dozen times. I couldn't get beyond the how-are-you, I-am-fine phase. Not sure what I wanted to say: marry me; go away; love me; forget me. I just didn't know.

If Mom longed for her only granddaughter, Dad was a different story. But then he'd always been a hard case. Not interested in little kids, including his own. But I'd noticed Mom couldn't hide the look in her eyes when she spoke of Emmy. She may not have ever liked Bree very much, but she couldn't resist the baby who looked so much like her son. I guess children have been bringing families together since humans first stood up on two legs. Since I knew about Emmy now, Mom was unabashedly keeping an eye on her and Bree and keeping me informed.

She wrote to say Bree was leaving Emmy with that damn John Carver during the day while she worked. I had to pace around camp for a while after I read that. What could Bree possibly see in that weasel? He didn't even have the guts to punch me back. Now he was taking care of my daughter and I was stuck in a hostile country on the other side of the world. There was no use in protesting to Bree, either by letter or phone. If she hadn't shown any interest in what I wanted when we were together, she sure wouldn't from a distance.

My unit was moving out on patrol and I struggled to bring my mind back to the world around me. Sand. Sand and rocks everywhere I looked. The heat was like a hammer beating on the top of my helmet. How could these poor schmucks bear to live here? Yet Afghan men walked with a proud swagger, broadcasting their satisfaction with their place in the world.

We moved warily along the narrow track surrounded by mountains. Cave mouths yawned above us, every one of them a possible hiding place for snipers. I kept looking up, feeling the hairs on my arms rise. Something felt hinky. The other guys felt it, too. I saw them all swiveling their heads, trying to look everywhere at once.

I heard the blast. I felt nothing.

~*~

"Mrs. Ketchum?" I said in surprise. I'd answered the door in my bathrobe, my head wrapped in a towel. It was early. Emmy was in her highchair, alternately beating her spoon on the tray and eating bites of scrambled egg. When the doorbell rang, Dad yelled at me to get it. And there was Billy's mother, wild-eyed.

"He's hurt. He's hurt bad," she said. "I hope you're satisfied! They came this morning, two officers, they came to the door and told us. He got blown up. I told him not to go into the Army. I told him...I told him..." She couldn't continue. Tears streamed down her face, but she didn't seem to notice them.

"Billy?" I said. "Billy's hurt?"

"What is it, Bree?" Dad called.

"And you're the reason!" Mrs. Ketchum said, her voice rising to a wail. "If it hadn't been for you, Billy'd still be here, working with his dad. You filled his head with ideas he never would've had. You made him as wild as you are. I blame you. I blame you!"

"But, but, will he be all right? He will be all right, won't he?" I asked in confusion.

Dad was there, putting his arm around me.

"Mrs. Ketchum, we are so sorry this has happened to Billy," he said. "May I drive you back home?"

She turned without another word and stumbled away.

I looked at Dad uncomprehendingly. "She said Billy's hurt bad," I whispered.

"Yes, honey, that's what she said." He hugged me tight, the way he used to when I was a little girl and came to him with my troubles. It used to be all I needed to make my troubles go away. It didn't work now.

I needed cash. It was all very well for the house's needs to be financed, but I had some needs of my own. Even little things like toothpaste and shaving cream cost money, and I had almost none. The rent money from my parents' house was held in escrow, so it would mean a trip back home and jumping through some legal hoops to get it. I'd rather do without. Bree offered to pay me for watching Emmy, but I wouldn't take anything for that. It was a privilege, that's the way I felt about it. And it was a way to stay in close contact with her.

Once again, I called Daw. He seemed to be my go-to guy for everything. "I need to make some money," I told him. "But I'm taking care of Emmy a few days a week now. Do you know of any jobs where I could work around that?"

"As a matter of fact, I was about to call you," Daw said, surprising me. "There's an old fellow named Guy Willet. I don't think you've met him, he doesn't get around much. He lives with his daughter-in-law. She teaches second grade – Marcie Willett."

"Oh, yeah, I met her at the party," I remembered. "Nice lady."

"That she is. Well, after Guy's son - Marcie's husband - died, Guy went downhill and she took him in to live with her. He goes to adult day-care at the community center, but he's confused. Gets his days and nights mixed up, wants to wander around at all hours. Marcie has to get up early and go to work, and she's not getting much sleep. She's worn out, poor soul. She's looking for somebody to stay with Guy at night. I thought of you, but I didn't say anything to her. Thought I'd kinda sound you out about it first."

"Well, yeah, that sounds like a possibility," I said. "I'd like to talk to her about it, anyway."

Daw made the arrangements and later that day, I stood on the front porch of the Willett residence. Colorful flower pots flanked the front door, which was painted bright red and sported a brass knocker. I knocked and Mrs. Willett answered, greeting me warmly and ushering me into the house. The living room looked just like the outside – pretty, clean and bright. Mr. Willett was sitting in a recliner, fast asleep.

"He was up most of the night," Mrs. Willett said, not bothering to keep her voice down. I guess she wasn't worried about waking him. "And of course, so was I. Since today's Saturday, it wasn't so bad. I got to sleep in until eight, which is the middle of the day for me."

"How can I help you, Mrs. Willett?" I asked.

"Please call me Marcie," she said. "I need someone to be here in the house at night when Dad gets up and wanders. Are you a sound sleeper?"

"About average, I think. I don't have trouble waking up, if that's what you mean."

"Do you think you'd hear him if you were asleep on the couch, say, and he got up and walked to the kitchen?"

"I think so. But you know, we could put an alarm on his door. I'd hear that, for sure. Or I could bring Queenie with me. She hears everything. She wakes for raindrops on the windowpane, and ice cubes falling into the icemaker tray."

"I think I'd prefer Queenie. That wouldn't scare Dad. He likes dogs. It might do him good to have one around sometimes."

We agreed that I'd show up on Sunday evening at 9 PM. Mrs. Willett – Marcie – could then retire to her bedroom, close the door, and sleep until morning secure in the knowledge that another adult was in the house, keeping watch.

Just then, Guy Willett woke. He stared at me unblinkingly for several minutes. I knelt by his side, introduced myself and shook his hand. I told him I'd be his buddy during the night if he woke up. We'd watch old movies on television, make popcorn, go for a walk, whatever he wanted. He nodded his head, but I didn't think he really comprehended. I looked at Marcie inquiringly.

"He'll be okay now," she said. "He may not remember who you are, but he seems to have a sense of having met someone before."

Sunday evening I arrived at the Willetts on time, my pillow in one hand, Queenie's leash in the other. I got a puzzled look from Guy, but Queenie got a big smile and a belly rub. Marcie went off to her bedroom, giving me only one backward glance and instructions to wake her if I needed her.

We settled down to watch Andy Griffith reruns. I noticed Guy's head immediately started nodding. I kept him awake with a steady stream of chatter, rubbing his shoulders, touching his arm, anything to keep him awake. I wanted him sleepy at bedtime. By eleven, he couldn't be kept awake any longer. I got him settled in his bed, then stretched out on the couch with Queenie on the floor beside me.

I felt Queenie's wet, cold nose brush my face. It seemed I'd just dozed off, but a look at my watch showed it was 4 AM. Guy was heading for the door in his pajamas. I made it there before him, turned him around gently and suggested we make a pot of cocoa. He looked perplexed, but sat quietly while I heated the milk. He drank his cup down, held it out for a refill, then headed to his recliner. Within fifteen minutes, he was snoring. I covered him with a blanket and lay back down, too.

Next thing I knew, Marcie was standing over me, whispering. "John. John, it's morning. You can go on home. I had the best night's sleep I've had in months – years! How was your night?"

"Not bad," I said, "Guy just got up once at four. He had a cup of cocoa and fell asleep again."

"That's because there was no pressure," Marcie said. "I'd have been trying to hurry him back to bed so I could get some sleep. You let him relax in his chair. Oh, John, I think this is going to work out. You can't know how much I needed help."

It became a regular thing that on weeknights, Queenie and I stayed at the Willett's. Some nights were more active than others, but I usually managed to get at least a few hours of sleep. If I needed to, I'd nap when Emmy did, if she did. Either that, or plenty of black coffee got me through the days. I made a little spending money and grew to genuinely like Guy Willett. He was old and confused, grieving still over the death of his son, and glad for some male company. I learned he used to play chess, so I brushed up on my knowledge of the game and we played nightly. We watched just about every old Western on the Movie Channel and consumed great bowls of buttered popcorn. Guy smiled more and greeted us happily when Queenie and I showed up. Marcie lost the exhausted, haggard look. It was going well.

If only my relationship with Bree had been going as well. Since she'd learned about Billy's wounds, I noticed she'd lost weight and jumped at every little sound. Emmy was still staying with her grandpa two days a week, and Bree mentioned it was an increasingly heavy burden for him.

"Bring her here every day, then," I said. "We've got a good routine going now. It wouldn't be any trouble."

"But you're working nights, too," Bree said. "When do you sleep?"

"I get some sleep at the Willett's, and I can catch up on weekends."

"I've been thinking...would it be easier or harder for you if Emmy and I moved in?" Bree asked.

To live in the same house with Bree! My heart leaped like it was about to exit my chest. I wanted to jump up and down and shout, but what I said was, "Oh, it'd be no problem if you were to move in."

"It's just that Dad's back is worse. He's seeing an orthopedic surgeon next week and may need surgery. It's not fair that he has to take care of Emmy while he's in so much pain. Mom is just being Mom, busy with everybody except her own family. I think it would be easier on them both if I moved out."

"Will they object to you moving in here – with me?"

"Yeah, they'll have a mini stoke apiece. But they like you and they know we're just friends."

That's how she felt? We're just friends? It was so far from my feelings that I felt my shoulders slump.

"It's time for me to make some changes," Bree went on. "Billy's coming home eventually, when he's better. I don't know what will happen between us then, but I need to get on with my life now."

"Do you think – I mean, are you thinking of marrying him?" I asked. It was hard to get a breath as I waited for her reply.

"I don't know," Bree said slowly. "I didn't say yes when he asked me, but now I'm questioning myself. He's Emmy's daddy; maybe I was being selfish for not making us a family. And now, of course, he...He'll need a lot of help."

"Emmy already has a family," I said. "And if you don't love

Billy, it won't work. But listen to me: what do I know about it? I just want you to do what you really want to do, not marry Billy out of pity."

"Yeah, you're right," Bree said. "But still...Billy was my first love. That never quite goes away, I think. He broke my heart, but now he needs someone. I just don't know what to do."

I could relate to the broken heart.

# Chapter Eight

Mom and Dad, predictably, had a fit. They worried about what people would say; they admonished me about making another mistake in a life filled, so far, with mistakes; they warned me that John and I might find we were incompatible house-mates. But in the end, they had no choice but to accept my decision to move into Uncle Charles' house. I think, secretly, they saw it as a more desirable alternative than marrying Billy. Mom took her frustration out on poor dead Uncle Charles.

"Damn the man!" she said. "Why did he have to leave such a crazy will?"

"I think he had something in mind, although I can't figure out what," I said. "In any case, I'm going to need the money from my half of the sale when the year's up. Meantime, I might as well take advantage of free housing. And admit it: you'll be glad to have your house to yourselves again."

The next Saturday, I loaded my car with what Emmy and I needed and we were off. John had the ground floor master bedroom, adjoining dressing room and bath sparkling clean. We set up Emmy's crib in the dressing room, I hung our clothes in the closet and we were moved. John and I looked at each other uncertainly. What now?

"Well, I guess I'll cut the grass," he said. "Supposed to rain tomorrow, and it's getting long. You and Emmy okay?"

"Of course. We'll... we'll...."

At that moment, Emmy tugged at my hand. "Out," she said. "Out."

"We'll go outside," I finished with a laugh.

The day passed with the usual Saturday chores. Laundry, errands, Emmy's meals and play times. As dinnertime approached, I wondered what to do about a meal. Was I supposed to cook and set the table, like we were a family? Or did we each fend for ourselves? My questions were answered by the aroma of frying bacon. I went to the kitchen to find John at the stove. Tomatoes, lettuce, mayonnaise, bread – he'd assembled the fixings for BLTs.

"Hey, would you slice those tomatoes?" he said over his shoulder as he carefully flipped the bacon.

Turned out, it was fun to assemble the meal together, put Emmy in her high chair and sit down at the table. We decided sometimes I'd cook, sometimes John would. Sometimes we'd order a pizza. Whatever, no big deal. It felt good to share a meal and discuss our day. We didn't lack for conversation, and much of it was punctuated with laughter.

We developed a routine. In the evenings, I'd get Emmy ready for bed and by the time she was asleep, John would leave for the Willett's. He'd return next morning to find Emmy up, dressed and fed, and me ready to head out the door for work. He'd take over Emmy's care until my return. Then supper and repeat. Our little household ran efficiently.

I kept waiting for the other shoe to drop.

It hurt, oh, my god, how it hurt. My legs burned with a thousand flames from the shrapnel, some of which was still there. I lay in Walter Reed Hospital doped to the gills, trying not to move any part of my body, especially my spine, which was broken in two places. It was too soon to know how much impairment I'd eventually have. I had to do some healing first. Getting out of bed was agony, but get me up they did, every day, talking about pneumonia and muscle atrophy. I sat in the bedside chair, fists clenched, gritting my teeth to keep from screaming.

After the first couple of weeks, the pain began to subside. I'd have a good day, followed by four bad days, then another good day. Mom and Dad visited once. It was a big deal for them to travel to Washington, D.C.; I knew that. They edged into my room, looking scared and shy and lost. Mom immediately burst into tears when she saw me. Dad harrumphed and looked away. I tried to think of positive things to say that might cheer them up.

"Well, looks like your baby boy will be coming home again," I said.

Mom grabbed onto those words like a lifeline. "Yes, and we'll get your old room all ready," she said, her eyes shining with purpose behind her glasses. "The social worker here, she said she'd help us learn what you need and how to take care of you. It'll be kinda like old times, won't it son?" She stopped, pressed her hand over her mouth and started babbling apologies.

"It's okay, Mom," I said. "It'll just be temporary, until I get well and can go back to active duty."

That only made her cry harder. I was relieved when they went back to their hotel, and even more relieved the next day when Dad said he needed to get back to work. I didn't have the energy to deal with my parents' emotional issues. I'd go back to their house when I was discharged. Then I'd figure out what to do next. Surely, Bree knew what had happened to me. She was bound to, in Grand Butte. The news would have spread all over town in an hour. I wondered when I'd hear from her.

~*~

I was surprised to hear Dr. Martin's voice on the phone. The ring had roused me from a quick nap. It hadn't been an easy night at the Willett's and I was trying to catch a few Zs while Emmy napped.

Dr. Martin said he'd just left the home of an elderly patient. He was the kind of doctor who still made house calls when necessary and he'd found this man in disarray and discomfort.

"He had a heart attack – a pretty bad one. He's recovering nicely, but he's still a little unsteady on his feet. The thing is, there's no one to look after him. His wife died a few years back, and they didn't have children. He's eating cereal for dinner, and stretching out the time between showers because he's afraid of falling when he's home alone. He needs companionship more than anything. I wondered if you could possibly look after him until he regains his strength."

"I'd be glad to, Doc, but I'm with Guy Willett at night and baby-sitting Bree's little girl during the day. I don't know when I'd be able to get over there."

"I know you have a full plate, John, but I've got an idea. That's a big house you're living in. Lots of bedrooms, lots of space. What would you think about my patient – his name is Carl Rothstein - moving in with you for a little while? Maybe a couple weeks, a month at most. He'd be able to pay, and he doesn't need much physical care. He mostly just needs company."

"I'd have to discuss it with Bree," I said. "Let me talk to her about it this evening and give you a call back."

"But John," Dr. Martin went on, "how do you feel about it? You'd be the one providing the care."

"If it was just up to me, I'd say yes right now. I like taking care of people. It's the one thing I'm fairly good at. But Bree gets veto power on this. It's her home, too."

Bree agreed immediately, almost casually. She knew Mr. Rothstein. He'd been the local pharmacist for years, one of those bedrock figures in a small town, willing to work with people who needed medicine but couldn't afford to fill their prescriptions until payday.

"As far as I'm concerned, he can move right into one of the upstairs bedrooms. That is, if he can manage stairs. That's something to ask Dr. Martin."

Ask I did, and was told Mr. Rothstein climbed stairs in his own home every day, an exercise considered part of his physical rehabilitation. On Saturday, when Bree was home with Emmy, I went to see him.

We were quickly on a first name basis. Carl was a sweet old guy, anxious not to cause anyone any trouble. He'd often been a guest in Charles' house, so he knew the size of the place. Still, he was afraid he'd be in the way.

"You'll have your own room and bathroom," I said. "We'll all eat together, but any time you want privacy, you can go to your room and close the door. One thing though - do you like little kids? Because Bree's daughter, Emmy, is only two."

"Love kids," Carl, said, his eyes lighting up. "Always wanted some of my own, but it didn't happen. Now I'm old, and wish

I had grandkids. I think I'd enjoy being around Emmy."

"She can be a pill," I warned him.

So can I." He grinned. "And I can always close my door, right?"

The transition went smoothly. I brought Carl over on Sunday afternoon and got him established in his room. He made slow work of the stairs, but he could do it. Emmy thought he was another grandpa and brought him a book to read to her as soon as he sat down. Bree was welcoming, but she didn't fuss over him.

"You're here to get stronger," she told him, "and I'm going to help you do that by not babying you, okay?"

"Okay," Carl replied. "Don't need babying."

And he didn't. That first supper, I grilled hamburgers and Bree made potato salad. Carl ate with great enjoyment.

"I can cook, too" he said, smiling at our surprised faces. "Haven't been doing it much lately, too much trouble to cook and clean up just for myself. But now, how about I make you one of my specialties? Do you have..." He rattled off a list of ingredients. Bree got a pad and pencil and after the dishes were done, she made a trip to the grocery store. The next evening we were treated to a gourmet meal. Carl suggested we put a sign-up sheet on the refrigerator, along with a running grocery list. Then whoever was cooking would be sure to have what was needed. We looked forward to Carl's nights at the stove.

We settled once again into a comfortable daily routine. I hung out within calling distance while Carl showered in the morning. During the day, he and Emmy and Queenie and I took long walks in the woods, where he could identify almost every plant we saw. After lunch he rested in his room. In the evening sometimes he'd watch television with Bree when I headed off to the Willett's. Emmy called him "gampa", which made Carl's whole face smile. We'd miss him when he went back home, and not just for the meals he cooked. He was a great guy.

Guy Willett, on the other hand, was sinking deeper into dementia. Sometimes he was combative, and poor Marcie took the brunt of it. Other days, he was mild but detached, off somewhere in his own world. His wandering grew worse. Marcie regained her gaunt look. I worried about her, but nights were all the time I could give her.

One day she collapsed at school. An ambulance took her to the hospital, where Dr. Martin examined her and said she was suffering from exhaustion and dehydration. He admitted her to the hospital for I.V. fluids, and ordered rest. Bree and I went around to see her.

"There's no place for Guy to go except a nursing home in the city," Marcie said, her face working. "He'll die there. I've got to be able to take care of him."

Bree and I exchanged glances. I raised my eyebrows; she nodded. I said, "Guy can come and stay with us for a while. Dementia patients do better in familiar surroundings, but he knows me and I think he'll be okay. I'll talk to Dr. Martin about adjusting his meds, and maybe put an alarm on his door so he can't slip away without my knowledge. You rest and catch your breath; we'll take care of Guy."

Guy was predictably thrown off course by the change in scenery and his daily routine. He wore a dazed expression that would have melted a harder heart than mine. Carl was good with him. They'd known each other all their lives, and somehow that still registered in Guy's diminishing brain. They spent long hours watching sports on television. Gradually, Guy got more comfortable. The biggest problem was his tendency to wander at night. I'd put him in the room next to mine, and hung a bell on his door knob. My sleep was interrupted many times by the tinkling sound I grew to hate.

Then I remembered something Papa Doc did for an inmate with dementia who couldn't be trusted to stay in the infirmary. I purchased a small, dark-colored round rug, which I put outside Guy's bedroom door. He looked at it warily and backed up. "Hole there," he said. That's what it looked like to him: a hole into which he could fall. He refused to cross it. During the day, I made the rug disappear, but it came back every night and kept Guy in his room.

It made me think about Papa Doc, wonder how he was doing, whether he was still at the prison. I wished I'd taken time to thank him for all he taught me, but most of all, for his kindness during the darkest time in my life.

John moved so fast, he was a blur. He basically worked day and night taking care of Emmy and our two boarders, but despite the crazy pace, he seemed to thrive. He walked taller, somehow. He said it was good to be needed.

Emmy loved being around her two new "gampas," but I wondered if all that adult attention was good for her. She had only to point at something and smile, and one of the men would get it for her. She was seldom cranky anymore. What would she have to be cranky about? Her days were filled with gratification. I wondered how she'd ever learn to cope with frustration, with the normal give and take between children. There weren't going to be any siblings any time soon, I was sure of that, and nursery school was still out of my reach financially. I didn't want to raise a little princess with a big sense of entitlement.

We were sleeping soundly one night – even Guy, by some miracle – when the town fire whistle shattered the nighttime quiet. Grand Butte didn't have a formal fire department, but dedicated volunteers were trained and ready to respond in an instant. In our little town, a fire meant everyone turned out. I could see the flames from the kitchen window. John stumbled downstairs, one arm in his shirt, shoes in hand.

"What is it?" he asked.

"Fire," I said briefly, tying my sneakers.

"Are you going?"

"Yes. Everyone goes," I said.

"Then let me," John said. "You stay here in case Emmy wakes up."

He was out the door and in his car before I could say yes. I went into the kitchen and filled the tea kettle;. It promised to be a long night.

I heard all about it afterwards, the townspeople repeating the stories like a Greek chorus. The old wooden apartment building, flames shooting to the sky, already burning like the eye of hell by the time help arrived. The fire fighters spraying water from the town's one tanker truck, neighbors using garden hoses and buckets. The apartment's residents, huddling in blankets, watching everything they owned feed the flames.

John jumped into the bucket brigade, passing heavy pails of water down the line. The building couldn't be saved, but the people who tried would always remember their team effort. John was part of that.

When he got back home at 4 AM, he wasn't alone. With him was a young woman, a baby girl and a little boy of about six, all of them covered with soot and dazed with exhaustion. I looked at them searchingly. Was it? Yes, it was Rosita. She'd been a couple of years ahead of me in high school, but we knew each other. I opened my arms to her, soot and all.

"I see you know each other," John said. "Hope it's okay I

brought them home. The Catholic Church opened their doors, but I didn't want the kids to have to sleep on those hard pews."

"Of course not," I said. "Rosita, you and your children are welcome."

"Oh, Bree, thank you," Rosita said. "I wouldn't put you to such trouble if it was just me, but the kids need a place to rest. This is Jamie and the baby is Isabella."

"What do you need first, something to eat, or baths?" I asked.

"Just water," Rosita said. "I don't think we could eat right now. Just water"

After they'd drunk their fill, I showed them to one of the upstairs bedrooms, the one with twin beds. We made a pallet on the floor for the baby, and I helped Rosita get the kids cleaned up. They had no clean clothes, so Jamie slept in one of my tee shirts, we put one of Emmy's just-in-case stash of diapers on little Isabella, and I lent Rosita a nightgown. By the time they were all tucked in, the sun was coming up.

I found John asleep at the kitchen table, his arms cradling his head. I rescued the tea kettle, boiled almost dry, and gave his shoulder a shake. "It's morning," I said.

He looked up blearily and somehow I just couldn't leave him with all the complications of the day ahead. "I'll call the bank," I said, "and stay home today. You go on to bed, get some sleep."

John didn't even protest. He nodded gratefully and plodded off to shower and bed. I called work. My supervisor was understanding. There'd been a fire, after all. But she said, "Bree, I need to warn you. You've been out of work a lot with one thing and another. It's really important that you improve your attendance. Do you know what I'm saying?"

"Yes, of course. Thanks," I said. I got it: even friend-of-your-daddy's jobs could be lost.

It was early afternoon when Rosita and the kids finally began to stir. John was still asleep when she came into the kitchen carrying Isabella, with Jamie clutching at her skirt. They still looked glassy-eyed with shock. I poured us cups of coffee and got Jamie a bowl of cereal. The baby ate dry Cheerios off Emmy's high chair tray. Rosita and I settled at the table.

"I can't thank you enough, you and Mr. Carver," Rosita began, "I can't believe you took us all into your home in the middle of the night."

"No thanks are necessary; we're glad to have you," I said.

We sat in silence for a few minutes. Then Rosita said, "I just got a job. It's at the diner. I'm a pretty good cook."

"Oh, then you'll be working with Patsy," I said.

"Yes, with Patsy. I was supposed to start next week."

"Well, you can still do that," I said. But Rosita shook her head.

"I don't see how," she said. "I was going to leave the kids with my neighbor, but now she's homeless, too. I must find a place to live, and get clothes and all the things we lost. It will cost money to replace just the bare necessities, and then I'll have no money to pay for child care."

"Look, don't worry too much about all that today," I said. "There are sure to be relief efforts going on right now – people will donate to help you and the kids. Just rest and let's see what happens."

Rosita took the kids, including Emmy, outside to play. Carl and Guy were already out there, Carl keeping a careful eye on Guy. Fortunately, Guy was having a cooperative day. I went upstairs and tapped on John's door. He was dressed except for his shoes, and he came downstairs carrying them in his hand, just as he had hours earlier when the fire alarm sounded.

I poured more coffee and let him drink it in peace. When he

looked more alert, I said, "John, I need to run an idea past you."

He looked up expectantly. I continued. "Rosita has a job cooking at the diner. She's to start next week. But now she has no place to live and no place for the kids to stay while she's working. I know there'll be scads of donated clothing and probably even a temporary place for them to live once the town gets organized, but day-care is going to be a problem. She had a neighbor who was going to watch the kids, but the fire took her home as well. So I was wondering. Would you be willing to look after her kids for a short time, until she can make other arrangements?"

He gave me an incredulous look. "Stay up half the night with a guy with dementia, then during the day, care for him and another man recovering from a heart attack, plus run after a two-year-old, then add a baby and another kid? I'm flattered; you must think I have superhuman powers."

Spelled out, it did sound ridiculous, and I felt my face grow hot. "I'm sorry. It wouldn't work out, I see that. Sorry for asking."

"It would be nice for Emmy to have kids her own age to play with," John said. "I wish I could do it, but even if I had the energy, there's something else: I can't take care of a stranger's kids. Think what Rosita would do if she found out about my past. You knew about it, you understood what happened before you entrusted Emmy to me, but this woman, she'd have me arrested. And who could blame her?"

I hadn't thought that far. John had a point, but his defeatist attitude made me angry. I suspected his zero self-esteem was curdling into self-pity. I took a deep breath to calm myself before speaking. It wouldn't do any good to make him feel defensive.

"I hear what you're saying, and I get it," I said. "But you're so burdened with the past, it's poisoning your present. You can't live your life because you worry all the time that you'll be found out, that you'll have to run away again. If it wasn't for Uncle Charles' will, you'd have been gone long ago, right?"

John nodded glumly. "I love it here," he said. "But I can't belong here, or anywhere, permanently."

"But what if you could? What if you could lay your burden down?" I asked. "Do you have the guts to do it? Or would you rather remain stuck in your "Poor John" mode?

That stung. I could see the hurt in his eyes. I felt like a sadist, but I had to finish what I'd started.

"What if you got in front of the story? What if you told it yourself? You could put it in context, tell the whole truth, rather than have people reacting to half-truths and suppositions."

"How would I do that?" he asked. "I can't call a town-hall meeting, or go door-to-door."

"Grand Butte has a grapevine that makes the Internet look like two tin cans attached by string," I said. "You'd just tell a few people and let them know it's all right to talk about it. By the next day, everybody will know."

"What if the reaction is what I expect? What if I get run out of town? Carl and Guy and Emmy depend on me."

"Nobody's going to get out the tar and feathers," I said impatiently. "Worst case, some folks react negatively – and probably some will. So they cross the street to avoid you, or pretend they don't see you in the grocery store. So what? Do you have to have universal approval to be okay? If you don't have it, does that mean you have to run away? Can you imagine holding your head up and going on with your life, no matter what other people think?"

John looked doubtful. I could see standing his ground was an idea he'd never entertained.

"I don't think you realize you're golden around here," I continued. "You came swooping in like Batman to rescue the local damsel in distress. Since then, you've cared for Uncle Charles and now Guy and Carl. Last night you stood with our neighbors and tried to save a burning building, for God's sake! You're the stereotypical good guy. Public opinion is squarely in your corner."

"Maybe at the moment it is," he said, "but even if you're right, parents aren't going to give a pass to someone they see as a predator."

"But that's where you make your case: you didn't abuse a child; you had consensual sex with a teenager who lied about her age. Those were the circumstances. You just need to explain it so people understand."

John stood up and paced around the kitchen. He looked out the window, but I knew he wasn't seeing the view. He paced some more.

"I need to think about this," he finally said. "I hate the idea of exposing myself to everyone. Ugh. Bad choice of words, but I mean, this is my private life. If I told someone, and I'm just saying if, who would I start with?"

"Daw."

But the next day, John was sick. He coughed until it seemed he'd turn himself inside out. Dr. Martin listened to his chest.

"Your lungs are compromised not only from smoke but from the chemicals in burning materials," he said. "There's nothing I can do except watch for a secondary infection like pneumonia. You're a healthy young man, and with a few days of rest and fresh air, you should be okay. But don't fool with this, John. It could get serious if you neglect it. I want you to stay in bed, you hear me?"

I called the bank to tell them I wouldn't be in for the rest of the week. My supervisor received the news with a clipped, "I see." I didn't even try to explain.

# Chapter Nine

I had plenty of time to think about what Bree said. She took over all the chores, including looking after Carl and Guy, while I lay around and coughed. I felt like a jerk, but Dr. Martin had been firm and I knew he was right. So I rested, and my mind churned.

All roads seemed to lead to Daw. It was he who made me stay in town after the accident, took me into his home, got me the job looking after Charles, presented me with the key to the city, endorsed me before his friends and neighbors. If it hadn't been for Daw, I'd have been far away from Grand Butte by now. I owed him a lot; it seemed a poor repayment to make him look like Barney Fife. For the truth was, if Daw had done his job as a lawman, had run a simple background check on me, he'd have booted me down the road himself.

After a couple of days of bed rest, I felt myself going stir-crazy. Carl and Guy were playing one of their endless games of poker and Emmy was engrossed in Sesame Street. I asked Bree if she could manage for a while if I took a walk, and when she said she could, I whistled up Queenie and headed into the woods.

Fear, shame, anger and distrust, all the bats that hung permanently in the rafters of my mind swooped down and flapped their wings. I was scared of having to leave this place even though I'd never expected to stay permanently. What made me sweat was the thought of leaving Bree. Being with her felt like I was home for the first time in my life. Emmy was exactly what I'd want my own little girl to be, the child I'd never have. I knew my feelings were not returned in kind. Oh, Bree liked me, maybe even loved me as a friend, but that's as far as it went. As for me, well, I'd miss them so much it made me sick to think about it.

I'd made commitments to care for Carl and Guy. I probably wouldn't be able to care for Guy much longer. He would gradually lose his ability to walk, to swallow food, to use the bathroom. Then he'd need twenty-four hour skilled care under a doctor's supervision. But until then, he was my responsibility. Carl would get better and go home, probably sooner rather than later, he was doing so well. But Guy wouldn't get better. I'd promised myself I'd make the days he had left as good as they could be, but if I had to leave town, Marcie would have no choice but to place him in care immediately.

Then there was the money. If I left before the year was up, as specified in Charles' will, I could kiss a sizeable inheritance goodbye. Worse yet, I'd screw it up for Bree, too. She was right; I needed to find a way to stay.

I tried to picture myself calling Daw, saying I needed to talk to him. I framed and discarded dozens of opening lines, but no amount of fancy talk could put lipstick on the pig that was my past.

Finally, I returned to the house with nothing resolved. I'd wait a few days, I decided, give myself time to get used to the idea. Maybe I'd practice on Rosita. She and her kids were still staying temporarily in the house. She had a right to know. Yes, I'd start with her, and there was no time like the present.

Rosita and Bree had the kids outdoors, playing in a little wading pool. The baby was sitting in the middle splashing energetically over the protests of the older kids. Screams of "Make her stop!" filled the air as Jamie and Emmy got wet.

"Hey!" I said, over the din. "Isn't getting wet the whole point? Get in there and play with her. Show her how to fill a pail. You're the big kids; you teach the baby."

Emmy considered this for a moment, and then she plunked down in the water beside Isabella. She held out the pink pail and a measuring cup from the kitchen. "Pour water," she said, demonstrating. Isabella watched carefully, then took the cup and tried it herself. Hardly any water went into the pail, but she crowed with glee and Emmy and Jamie laughed, too. Peace was restored. Or as much peace as can be found with three little ones.

Bree and Rosita mimed applause from their shady spot on the patio. I joined them.

"You have a good way with them," Rosita said shyly. "I don't know how I can ever thank you both for taking us in. I hope we won't be in your way too much longer."

This was my opening. "Rosita," I said, "there's something I need to tell you."

Bree made a move to leave, but I said, "No, please stay, Bree." I launched into my story. I hadn't rehearsed it mentally and made no attempt to polish it up. I tried to be as objective as possible and stick to the facts. Rosita listened without a word. When I finished, I invited her to ask me anything.

She said, "So you were eighteen and your girlfriend was

fifteen, right?"

"Right," I said.

"And you thought she was older because she lied about her age. Then her Dad blamed everything on you and had you thrown in jail."

"Yes, that's what happened. I'm responsible for my actions, though. I think my punishment was too harsh under the circumstances, but I did my time and that's behind me. What will never be behind me is public opinion when people hear the word 'pedophile.'"

"You aren't that," Rosita said, shaking her head. "Whatever mistakes you made – bad judgment or whatever – you didn't molest a child. If I thought you had, I'd pick up my kids and leave this minute, even if we had to go sleep on those church pews."

"Do you think of me differently though, now that you know?" I asked anxiously, waiting once again for judgment. Bowing to the verdict of others was a hard habit to break.

"I guess I do," she said. "Now, I know you are carrying a heavy burden without complaining or making excuses, so I like you even more."

At that moment, Jamie threw the big plastic beach ball and knocked Isabella over sideways. She screamed and Rosita jumped up to rescue her. Emmy started crying in sympathy, and Jamie joined her. Into the pandemonium moseyed Guy and Carl, tired of their game and looking for distraction. There'd be no more serious conversations today. Bree and I exchanged a glance and she nodded. My shirt was soaked under the arms, and I realized I was shaking, but I'd done it: I'd told someone.

Next, Daw.

I put it off until it was more painful to dread it than just do it. When that moment came, about eight o'clock one evening, I drove over to Daw's house. Didn't call to see if he was home or if it was convenient, I just went. He was in the garage, working on his lawn mower. Both the mower and Daw were upside down, both were covered in grass clippings and oil, and both were sputtering.

When he saw me standing in the doorway, he stood up clutching his lower back, and said, "Thank God! It was going to be me or the damn mower, and I think I'd have lost. What can I do for you?"

I told him I needed to talk to him, and my face must have told its own story. He nodded, wiped his hands on an old shop rag and led the way to the screened porch.

"Janey went to see her sister," he said. "No telling when she'll get home. They forget they're two grown women when they get together. Such giggling and carrying on. Can I get you a beer?"

I said I'd love one, and popped the top off the cold can he brought me. A little Dutch courage for the task ahead.

"So, what's up?" Daw asked.

"Well, I need to tell you something," I began. "It's hard to know where to begin. See, there's something in my past you need to know about."

I stopped, searching for words. Daw looked at me steadily.

"You mean your conviction for statutory rape and your time in prison? I wondered when you'd feel like telling me about it."

"You knew? You knew and never said anything?"

"'Course I knew. You think I'd invite some stranger to sleep in the same house as my wife and not know anything about him? I ran your name the night of the accident and read the whole case file on the database. Next morning I called the prosecutor and your public defender. They had remarkably similar stories to tell – young guy, got in over his head with a girl, fell for a lie, took the brunt of her Daddy's rage, drew a hard-nosed judge who showed no mercy. Think you're the first guy that's happened to? Hell, it could've been me if Janie was another kind of girl."

I just stared at him. Could I be a bigger chump? Daw had been wise to me all along, ready to jump in and collar me if I screwed up again. And I'd been thinking my big secret was safe. Anger rolled in like a hot tide. I felt the muscles in my jaw jump as I clenched my teeth.

"Told Charles, of course," Daw continued. "Wouldn't have let you in his house without him knowing. He was a pretty astute old guy. Sized you up in that first meeting and gave me the high sign. After that, I just waited to see how things turned out. Never saw anything that gave me the least bit of concern, John, you need to know that. You've proved yourself over and over."

Slowly, the anger receded, and in its place came gratitude. I'd been hanging on to my secret so hard, hiding it away like a crazy old uncle in the attic. But Daw had known, had carefully checked me out, decided he trusted me, and allowed me find my own way. It reminded me of Sam's watchful guidance when I was a kid, and Papa Doc's while I was in prison. I realized that, while I'd had some bad luck in my life, I'd also had some extraordinarily good luck in father figures. I blinked hard and looked away, embarrassed by the tears in my eyes, but Daw didn't seem to notice. He stood and went in the house, saying he needed another beer, giving me a chance to collect myself.

"So what do you want to do now?" he asked, settling back down, popping the cap on his beer. "I'm guessing you came to me because you're tired of being scared and feeling like shit about yourself, right?"

"Right! It'd be great to not always be waiting for that tap on my shoulder. Bree says I should tell people myself."

"Yeah, I know. We talked. I went to tell her about you before she moved into Charles' house. Didn't think it was fair not to. But she said you'd already told her. We decided to let you figure things out for yourself."

"She gave me a kick in the pants," I said, "asked me if I wanted to be Poor John for the rest of my life, or if I had the guts to own my past. It hurt, I'll admit it. But I thought about it, and she was right, as usual. So here I am. What do I do next?"

"Why don't you let me take care of the next couple of steps?" Daw said. "I'll get the word out, low-key, you know, tell the whole story, not just the headlines. People know you by now, they've gotten used to you. Let's see what happens.

In the next few days, I noticed a few people avoided me. They suddenly didn't see me in the grocery store or on the street. It bothered me, of course. I wanted to be liked. But it helped that others – men, mostly – wrung my hand and thumped me on the shoulder, conveying their support without saying much. Bree said the whole town was buzzing for a while, but even sensational stories have a sell-by date, and mine seemed to expire on schedule. I knew a whiff of suspicion would always be attached to me, never completely forgotten, but on the whole, acceptance was much better than I'd anticipated. I was still here. I hadn't run.

Bree lost her job about then. She said the bank manager called her into his office and said she'd been absent so much they had to replace her with someone more dependable. Nothing wrong with her work, he said, the bank simply needed someone who would show up every morning and work all day. Bree thanked him for giving her a chance, cleaned out her desk and came home bearing a celebratory bottle of supermarket champagne.

"To fresh starts," she said. We clinked our glasses.

Then she didn't know what to do with herself. Her housing was taken care of, thanks to Charles, but she, too, needed spending money. We still had Rosita and her kids staying at the house until the end of month when their new apartment would be available. Bree and Rosita worked out an arrangement. For a nominal fee, Bree would care for Isabella and Jamie along with Emmy, while Rosita worked at the diner.

Bree made it into a real job. She didn't just plunk the kids in front of the T.V. or put them out in the backyard to play. The kitchen blackboard held a schedule with an activity for every hour of the day, from finger-painting to nature walks to rest time. Even baby Isabella participated as much as she could, and when she couldn't, Bree carried her in a sling on her back. It was a full day and by evening, Bree was tired but happy. She'd discovered her passion, she said, and it was caring for kids.

An old high-school friend heard about it and asked Bree if her two-year-old could join the group. Then another, and another. Bree now spent her days looking after six kids ranging in age from one to four. It was exhausting work, but she loved it.

Carl and Guy thrived on all the activity. I'd worried that the noise and commotion of little kids would drive them crazy, but the opposite seemed to be true. On his bad days, Guy might stay in his room more, but most of the time, both men wanted to be where the action was. Bree was grateful for whatever help they could offer, and the kids took to them with the natural affinity between young and old.

Watching the interaction between my guys and Bree's kids, an idea formed in my mind, so new and nebulous I didn't want to put it into words yet for fear of killing it still-born. I'd read a bit about how the old and young benefited from contact with each other and I was intrigued. What if, I asked myself as I waited for sleep at night, what if Bree and I could form complimentary small businesses based here at the house? She'd look after children; I'd look after elderly men. We'd offer daycare at each end of the generational spectrum.

We actually had a small version of that going on right under our noses. The kids called Carl and Guy grandpa. While Guy didn't respond to much of anything anymore, he did smile at that. Carl ate it up. He thought he'd missed his chance at grandchildren forever, and was delighted with the kids. Isabella especially touched his heart, and she loved him back. Nap time always meant a long session in the old wooden rocker, with Carl singing tuneless songs and Isabella snuggling in his arms. He asked me if he could still come back after he moved home, just to see the kids. It'd give him something to look forward to, he said. Of course he could, I said, he'd always have a warm welcome here.

I developed an informal plan. I figured I could look after three or four elderly gentlemen who would arrive in the morning and spend the day, with maybe one or two staying with us for respite care. No crabby old guys who only wanted peace and quiet; they'd have to enjoy kids. Bree's play-group would prosper, I felt certain. We knew from our own experiences that Grand Butte sorely lacked affordable resources for these age groups. If we charged even half of what such services would cost elsewhere, we'd come out with an adequate income, and we'd be doing work we loved. I decided to talk to Dr. Martin about it, get his feedback. Maybe I'd overlooked something he could point out.

He answered the door in his slippers and shirt sleeves when I knocked later that evening. Mrs. Martin was knitting in the living room and she smiled warmly as I entered.

"John! What a nice surprise. Come in and sit down. Can I get you something to drink?" she said.

"Sit still, dear, I'll get John some iced tea. How's that cough?"

After a few minutes of small talk, I launched into the reason for my visit. They listened silently.

"I'm sure you've heard about my past." I said, and they both nodded. "Do you think it would prevent us from offering the kind of home care I'm proposing?"

"Depends on whether you plan to file for a business license for either enterprise. Bree couldn't get a childcare license with a convicted felon in the house. You couldn't get an elder-care license for the same reason," Dr. Martin said.

I appreciated his bluntness. Might as well tell it like it is. But I felt the familiar discouragement descending. Here was another roadblock thrown up by my past. Not only was I standing in my own way, I was standing in Bree's as well. I'd have to leave town the minute the year was up, leave Bree and Emmy and any chance for happiness with them. I knew I deserved every crappy thing that happened in my crappy life. The old panicky urge to cut and run came on strong.

Dr. Martin was still talking. "But this is a very small town, and we don't necessarily observe all the formalities. If you and Bree were to offer neighborly services to friends – and that's just about everyone in a town this size – it'd be a different story. The biggest stumbling-block to such an informal arrangement is that people might not be able to claim the child-care deduction on their tax returns. But perhaps if they were getting good care at an affordable price, they'd feel it was worth it. Bree could concentrate on younger children, about Emmy's age, for whom daycare costs the most. As for elder-care, Grand Butte simply doesn't have any. I know of three men right now who are in great need of that kind of service. I'd love to be able to recommend a solution for their families."

His calm voice quieted my panic a little. He was trying to help and I made an effort to respond.

"Carl and Guy have been easy," I said. "Even Guy, although he's getting to the stage now where I won't be able to keep him much longer. Carl has made great progress and is ready to go home, but he says he doesn't want to. He likes living with other people, interacting with the kids every day, having good meals, and structure for his days."

"Well, that's another option you might consider: offering a home to men like Carl. They'd pay, of course, for your time and a share of expenses. It's something to think about," Dr. Martin said. "I'm wondering though, is what I heard true, that you and Bree have to occupy Charles' house for a year before you can sell it? It'd be a shame to get people's hopes up, get them accustomed to counting on you and Bree, and then sell out."

"I hadn't thought that far," I admitted. "Bree and I haven't talked much about what will happen when the year's up. I guess we're still young enough that a year seems like a long time to us. That's something we'll need to discuss. The next step is talking to Bree. She may veto the whole idea."

~*~

I loved the idea. Offering services to young and old on a business-like basis answered the questions plaguing me about my immediate future. I regretted not having gone to college. Much as I loved my daughter, I regretted getting my MOM degree 'way too early in life. If I had a marketable skill, if I was qualified for a career of some kind, I'd have more options. When I tried to look ahead into Emmy's and my futures, I could only see a brick wall.

But now, here was something I loved to do, caring for children. A group of six kids was just the right size for me to handle. Isabella was the only baby, but I hoped to add at least one more infant when I had more experience under my belt. It might mean taking on help, but I'd deal with that when the time came.

I woke before the alarm clock every morning, eager for the coming day. The sight of those little faces brought me joy. With a houseful of kids there were sure to be rough spots, but that didn't discourage me. I planned a full day of simple activities because busy, engaged children are good children.

Emmy blossomed. Who knew my little daughter had such a social side? She thrived on the give and take of the group, no longer expecting to point, smile and receive. Now she had to negotiate with the other kids for what she wanted.

John fretted about our lack of licensing. I told him to lighten up and remember he was in Grand Butte. Since his secret lay bare for all to see, potential clients could judge for themselves which carried more weight: a man they'd come to know and respect, or a past misstep with harsh consequences. Marcie Willett approached me about it.

"John is just wonderful with Guy," she said, tapping my arm for emphasis. "I understand completely what happened to him as a teenager. I'm an old school teacher and I've seen it all. But that was then, and this is now. John has proved himself to my satisfaction. I'm telling people I'm proud to trust him with Guy's care."

I decided to call my kids a play group. It sounded more fun and less formal than day-care, and besides, that's what we did all day – play. Often the play concealed lessons, like the spoonful of sugar that made the medicine go down. Emmy was counting, not just reciting the numbers, but actually counting objects up to ten. Jamie was sounding out words in books. Isabella was starting to talk, urged on by the older kids she tried her best to emulate.

John had all the clients he could possibly say grace over as word spread. Beleaguered households gratefully learned that respite care was available for their elderly. They brought Grandpa to stay for a day or a week. The elderly gentlemen often arrived reluctantly, suspicious of new things, disoriented by change. John would soon have them involved in a shared activity and after they'd had a good meal and lively conversation, they settled in. Most of them loved interacting with the children; those that didn't could have all the peace and quiet they wanted in their upstairs sitting room, which was off-limits to my kids. Grudge-match checker games and killer dominoes tournaments were played there, and there was always a big jigsaw puzzle spread out on a table, away from little hands. John began saving up to install a chair lift on the stairs for those who found the climb difficult.

Carl decided to make our home his home. He put his house on the market, and when it sold within a week, he told us we were stuck with him now. John gave him a slap on the back and said we couldn't get along without him.

I went home one evening to see how my Dad was getting along after his back surgery. The house was spotless, the patient was ensconced comfortably on the sofa reading a book, and delicious smells wafted from the kitchen. Dad beamed when he saw me.

"You wouldn't believe how well I'm doing, Bree," he said. "The physical therapist says I'm the poster boy for back rehab. Only thing is, your Mom is cooking me such great meals, I'm going to get too fat to exercise."

Mom actually giggled. "Oh, now!" she said, and happily puttered back to the kitchen to watch what was on the stove. Obviously, some romance had crept back into their relationship now that they had the house to themselves again.

Mom caught me up on all the Grand Butte gossip, including news of Billy. I'd been so busy I'd hardly spared a thought for him. Mom said he was back home, living with his parents.

"No one sees him much," Mom said.

"Do you think I should go see him?" I asked.

Both my parents looked surprised that I'd ask their advice. Certainly I'd not listened to anything they had to say about Billy in the past.

"Well," Mom said, pleating the dishtowel between her fingers, "it might be the right thing to do, under different circumstances. But, Bree, I don't want you to get mixed up in all his troubles."

I felt the familiar stir of resentment at being given orders about my emotional life, but reminded myself I was no longer a rebellious teenager. "His troubles include a broken back and legs full of shrapnel," I said mildly. "If he was an old friend, I'd be asking what I could do to help him. It shouldn't be any different."

"But it is," Mom said. "He's Emmy's father. What if he wants to be part of her life – part of your life? What would you do then?"

~*~

I had to repress the urge to go on the hunt for something to take the edge off. I remembered the places a guy could buy dope in this little town. Pot might have given me some relief when the pain was at its worst,. Eventually it settled down - still there, but bearable. I could get by with just a few aspirin a day.

 What was worse was the pain in my mind, the nightmares. Over and over, I relived the flash of the explosion. I remembered hearing the boom, the boom that still reverberated through my head. If Mom dropped a pan, I jumped a mile. If Dad slammed the door, I came up out of my chair ready to fight. Once, dozing on the couch, I woke from the familiar nightmare to see a dim figure looming over me. Despite my bad back, I shot to my feet swinging, and knocked poor Mom across the room. The purple bruise on her cheek reminded me for a couple of weeks what a miserable human being I'd become. Awake, the bad vibes buzzed inside me, but I could control them. Asleep, all my demons came out to play. I tried to stay awake as much as possible.

So those were my nights, imprisoned in my boyhood bedroom with the cowboy wallpaper, and now Mom's sewing machine in the corner. My days were spent doing physical therapy, icing my back, and watching television with my folks. Sure, I was glad to be alive, but was this what my life was going to be now?

I'd never been a reader, so I found no escape in books, not that there were any in my parents' house. Even T.V. was a very limited commodity. No cable, just the three networks and one of them was fuzzy. There was one television set so we sat together on the sofa to watch it like birds on a wire.

My buddies from high school came around the first couple of days I was home. They were all married now, with families. They looked ill at ease and had trouble making conversation after they'd fist-bumped and thanked me for my service. One by one, they cited families waiting at home, supper on the stove, yards to mow, sick babies, anything to provide them with a reason to get up and walk out. I envied those walks out. Would have done the same thing if I could. They didn't come back. Probably figured they'd done their duty, busy lives and all. I didn't blame them.

Baby steps measured my progress – literally – but I could now walk short distances without a cane. My spine felt like a column of fire, but I tried to focus on my goal of driving again. Dad had a truck and Mom had an old car; I could practice in them. If I could get in a car and go somewhere, maybe I wouldn't feel the stifling claustrophobia. Meanwhile, I stopped shaving and bothering with haircuts, didn't pay too much attention to personal hygiene, and spent most of my time in gym shorts. Couldn't stand for long pants to touch my legs where the shrapnel wounds still festered. The shorts' elastic waistband accommodated the gut I was developing from too much of Mom's cooking and not enough exercise. So I was a hot mess on the day Bree dropped by.

She looked terrific. Tan, tall, slim, smelled good, too. Slumped in my chair, I had a flash of how I must appear to her. I didn't stand. I couldn't meet her eyes. Bree dipped down to kiss my cheek, wrinkling her nose as she got a whiff of me.

"Geez, Billy! You could use a shower," she said, and at that moment she was so much like the old Bree that we both laughed. It was my first laugh in a long time.

"Yeah, I know. I know," I said. "It's hard to do and just doesn't seem worth the effort."

"Well, if you're aiming at a new career as a scarecrow, you're on the right path," she said. "How are you? Really."

"Really? I'm in pain, I'm depressed, I'm worthless and I wish I was dead," I said.

"Not to mention wallowing in self-pity," she said remorselessly. I'd forgotten how tough she could be. "You have a daughter, remember? She might like to know her daddy, now that you're home."

"I have nothing to offer a kid," I said, "or anybody else, for that matter. Why don't you just go back to your big house and your new boyfriend and leave me alone?"

Bree cocked her head. "What, now? I may get half a big house eventually, but right now I'm baby-sitting kids and living with several nice room-mates, although they are rather ancient. John's not my boyfriend, but he is a good friend. You ought to get to know him. In fact, you ought to come over sometime, hang out with all of us. Get out of here for a while."

"No, thanks!" I responded. "I'm not that desperate."

"You look pretty desperate to me," she said. She had a way of looking straight through me. "In fact, you look miserable. Why don't you come home with me right now?"

"Now? No. Why don't you bring Emmy here to see me?"

"Nope, not comfortable with that. Your parents have shown no interest in her in two years. I'm not going to make it easier for them now."

"You're being pretty hard on them," I said.

"Yeah. It's been hard for everyone. Look, tomorrow get yourself cleaned up and I'll be here to get you at ten. John and the guys can watch the kids for a few minutes while I'm gone. You can have lunch with us, and then when it's time to put the kids down for naps, I'll bring you back."

"It's not a good idea, Bree," I said. "I'll scare the kids."

"They'll be curious because you're a stranger, then they'll ignore you. That's the beauty of kids – they accept whatever they see and move on."

She was walking toward her car, speaking over her shoulder, and then she was gone. I didn't have a chance to protest any more. Mom spoke from behind the screen door.

"You don't have to go with that wild girl, Billy," she said in the same tone she'd used when I was in first grade. "You just stay here where you're safe. No telling what she'd get up to. You just stay here with me."

She sealed the deal, you might say. At that moment, I became determined to be ready when Bree came for me the next day.

I woke up at six and started on my rehabilitation as a human being. Taking a shower required that Dad stand by in case I lost my balance. I had to catch him before he went to work. After that, I sat against an ice pack a while, drank several cups of coffee and ate some dry toast to settle my stomach. The pain was nauseating, but I was determined not to take a pill. I pressed on, squinting into the mirror to shave. I couldn't do anything about the haircut I needed, but resolved to get to Ed's Barber Shop as soon as possible. I felt better, and except for the little flags of toilet paper stuck to the places I'd cut myself, I looked better.

Clothes were a problem. Nothing fit but those damn gym shorts and I didn't want the kids to see the angry red scars on my legs. Mom finally unearthed an ancient pair of washed-soft sweatpants with a draw-string waist that I could let out to the max. I made a silent promise to lay off the fried steak and gravy. Ignoring the tenderness of my still-healing skin, I slipped into a clean white tee-shirt, and I was as ready as I'd ever be. I was exhausted, but also – well, excited, I guess would be the word. I hadn't been off the place since I got home. I wasn't thinking about seeing my daughter; just about not seeing the same four walls.

Mom didn't try to hide her disapproval. When Bree arrived, she made herself scarce, which meant Bree had to help me into the car by herself. It was an awkward business because I couldn't bend my back much. Like robo-man, I lowered myself inch by inch into the car seat, smacking my head in the process. Fortunately, we both got to laughing at the same time and it was okay.

The road to Charles' house was the same one on which she'd had her accident. When she got to the spot, she slowed down and told me about it.

"I can't remember the crash itself, just waking up in the front seat and seeing John standing beside the car. I could hear Emmy saying 'Mama,' but I couldn't see her. The car was creaking and shimmying. I thought for sure I'd go over with it. All I could think of was Emmy. Then John pulled us out and the car went down."

I cleared my throat. "Look, about John. I'm sorry I clocked him that time in Charles' yard. It was just reflex, you know. Saw him kissing you and all."

"It's not like that between us," Bree said. "He's a great friend. My best friend, I guess, but he's like a brother. That kiss was just a one-off."

For you, maybe, I thought, but I didn't say it. No point in getting into an argument. Besides, who was I to be jealous? I'd forfeited that right a long time ago. Bree owed me nothing.

When we pulled into the driveway at Charles' old house, John was waiting. "Carl's watching the kids in the play yard," he said to Bree. Then he stuck out his hand. "John Carver," he said. "I don't think we exchanged names the last time we met."

And damned if he didn't give me a big grin. I shook his hand and accepted his help out of the car. When you lose your mobility, you gain a certain humility. John was giving Bree an update on what had happened in the few minutes she'd been gone, which seemed to have been quite a lot. She was laughing, and describing her struggles to get me here. They talked to each other like an old married couple – or maybe a brother and sister. I felt the knot between my shoulder blades relax a little.

And there she was, my daughter. She was bossing the other kids around, directing them in building some kind of fort out of big cardboard boxes. What she lacked in language, she made up in authority. "No, Timmy, you wait!" she said, and a little boy obediently backed off. She was small. I didn't know if she was small for her age, but she looked tiny to me. Bree had put her hair in two wispy pony tails that stuck out from the sides of her head. The ribbon bows had come undone and flapped around her fierce little face. She didn't spare me a glance.

I felt something turn over in my heart. This was my little girl. Bree's and mine. I could have looked at her all day. John helped me lower into a lawn chair, slipping a cushion behind me to keep my back straight, and I watched the kids play. After a while, one of the little boys noticed me and came over to see who I was.

"Hey, mister," he said.

"Call me Billy, okay?"

"Mister Billy?" he said dubiously. Apparently, he'd been taught not to first-name adults.

"Yeah, okay, Mister Billy is fine," I said.

He nodded, taking in my stiff posture. "Are you a robot?" he asked in a whisper.

"Nope, but I'm having a little trouble getting around right now," I said.

He regarded me silently. By now, all the kids were standing in a semi-circle around me. They peppered me with questions, which I answered as honestly as I could: I had a bad accident with a lot of boo-boos, but the doctor fixed me up; yes, I can walk, but no, I can't run, not yet. I told them I bet they could run really fast, and asked them to show me. Emmy was right there among them and it made me feel good to see her little legs pumping as she tried her best to beat the boys.

Bree gave me a wink and a smile when she came to call the kids to lunch. She'd spread it all out on the picnic tables and everyone, even the little kids, found a seat and dug in. The sturdy plastic plates held fresh fruit, a grilled cheese sandwich and a handful of corn chips. Desert was popsicles, which turned everyone technicolored in no time. John was right there, wiping chins and replacing spilled juice cups. The old guys were there, too, having the same lunch as they chatted with the kids. One of the men seemed pretty out of it. He didn't talk much, just smiled vaguely. John sat down beside him and tore his sandwich into tiny bites, watching carefully as each bite went down. When the old guy was finished, John wiped his chin as matter-of-factly as he did those of the children. I was beginning to like John. Didn't expect that.

Billy wasn't actually too bad. He'd lost that cocky swagger and seemed more human and less threatening. I liked the way he interacted with the kids. And when Carl thanked him for his service, I liked that Billy asked him if he'd served. Carl said yes, in Korea, and they talked about Army life. Bree didn't pay any more attention to Billy than to anyone else; in fact, she treated him like one of the kids. I had no sense of sparks flying between them, and that was reassuring.

When the kids went down for naps, I offered to take Billy home. Bree thanked me, allowing as how she wouldn't mind putting her feet up for a few minutes. Billy's face fell a bit, but he said that would be fine. I helped him into my car and followed his directions to his parents' house. We rode in silence for a few minutes.

Then he said, "Emmy seems to have forgotten our first meeting."

"Yeah, kids don't remember stuff for long," I replied.

"Look, I owe you an apology," he said. "I'm sorry for punching you."

"No problem, man," I said. "It's forgotten."

"One thing, though, before we forget it ever happened," Billy said. "I was jealous when I saw you kissing Bree. Now you're living together, but she says that's a matter of convenience. I need to know: is there anything between you and Bree?"

I felt a flash of irritation. Where did this guy get off, to think he could question me about the most private and personal matters? I schooled my voice carefully. Billy'd been through a lot. He could be forgiven for lack of tact.

"Bree has no romantic feelings for me that I can tell," I said.

"So she said. But how do you feel about her?" He was relentless.

I turned my head to meet his eyes. "I love her," I said. It felt good to say it out loud. "But I don't want to lose her as a friend, so I don't push it. Maybe someday, she'll, I don't know, change in how she feels about me."

Billy nodded briefly. He looked out the side window. It seemed our conversation was over. Then he said, without looking at me, "If you want her, go after her. Don't be so afraid to go after what you want."

I thought about Billy's advice a lot that night. He was right. I was afraid to go after what I wanted because I was convinced I didn't deserve it. If even Billy could see it after just a few hours with me, it must be glaringly obvious to those who knew me better. To Bree. She was the only person whose opinion really mattered.

But I didn't dare rock the boat. Things were going so well, she with her play group, and me with my old guys. I had a home, if only until the year was up. How could I risk all that? Besides, Bree had apparently told Billy she had no romantic feelings for me. Couldn't be clearer. It would be best if I put aside my feelings for her, yet how could I, living in the same house? When the year was up, I'd leave, that's all. Just get out and keep going. A part of me always wanted to cut and run. A bigger part yearned for stability, home and family. I waged a familiar war with myself, but as usual, there was no winner. It was late when I finally slept.

The next morning, we were back to status quo. My old guys wanted their coffee just the way they liked it, then they wanted to read the newspaper in peace, and then they wanted to go outside, sit in the sunshine and watch the kids play. Bree's kids wanted to have a food fight over breakfast ("No!"), finger-paint with their eggs ("No!") and play outside ("Yes!"). It all worked out. Same old, same old. Only today I felt different, energized.

When there was a lull in all the activities, Bree asked me what I'd thought of Billy. I struggled for an honest, but tactful answer.

"He seems to have changed," I said tentatively.

"Well, yeah. His injuries would change a person," Bree said. "Do you think he's depressed?

" How could he not be?"

"But, do you think… Oh, I don't know what to think," Bree said, running her hands through her hair in frustration.

"Look, I hardly know the guy. He punched me in the nose at our first meeting. Yesterday he apologized for that. So I'm neutral, like Switzerland. Why does my opinion matter to you?"

"I guess because I'm trying to figure out how I feel about him now," Bree said. "When he was home before, he was so full of himself, so bossy. I didn't like him much. But now he's vulnerable. When we were kids, I'd see the boy he really was under the tough guy facade. That's what I loved, and that's what I see again. It kind of tugs at my heart."

I nodded, ignoring the pain her words brought. She needed a good listener, and I was determined to be whatever Bree needed.

"And he's Emmy's daddy," Bree went on. "That counts for a lot. I almost feel, I don't know, obligated to give him a chance with her."

"And with you?"

"Kinda goes together," Bree said.

My heart sank.

~*~

Looked like they had it all together, John and Bree. There was so much going on in that house I only felt like a stranger for the first few minutes. It's hard not to get involved with little kids, they draw you right in. My daughter was the smartest and cutest of all of them. Pint-sized, assertive, struggling to express herself with words that were still new, she was a dynamo. The other kids deferred to her, even though some of them were older. Make a good Army officer, I thought.

I missed Army life. I'd planned to make it a career. I wasn't even thinking of twenty-and-out and the pension; I wanted to stay in the Army all my working life, get a college degree, go to officers' training school and make rank. That route was all there in my head, and everything I'd done pointed in its direction. I expected to go back to active duty, yearned for it. But first I had to get myself back in shape. I redoubled my efforts in PT and started pushing Mom's plates of food away. Job one: get rid of the gut. Job two: learn to sleep without the nightmares.

My folks weren't much help. Well, that's not accurate. They did everything they could think of to help me, but they were limited by their own lack of experience in the big, wide world. Grand Butte had been their only home. They'd lived their entire married life in the same house. Dad worked at the same place since he graduated high school. All they could think of, especially Mom, was keeping me safe, feeding me, and plumping pillows behind my aching back. What I knew for sure was I didn't want to spend the rest of my life like that.

There was one person who always gave me an honest opinion, who didn't feel sorry for me, and who'd given me some pretty good pep talks in the past: Bree. I felt a compelling need to talk to her. Just the two of us, like old times.

I called her and she agreed to come over the next day, which was Saturday. I picked a time when Mom would be doing the grocery shopping so we'd have some privacy. Once again, I rose early and struggled to make myself presentable. Bree arrived on the dot, swinging out of her car and striding up to the porch where I waited.

"I don't have much time," she said. "John is looking after Emmy."

"You could have brought her along," I said. "I'd have liked to see her."

"You said you needed to talk – there are no conversations with that kid around," Bree said, laughing. "You may have noticed she likes to do all the talking herself. So what's up?"

It poured out of me: frustration and anger and pain, self-pity I'd tried to conceal, fear for my future, the nightmares, it all fell in a nasty pile at Bree's feet. She held my eyes the whole time, never flinching. Bree always had a great heart. She put her arms around me, and I felt that heart beating next to mine.

"Billy. It will be all right," she said softly. "You'll be okay. You'll get your life back."

She offered no solutions, only a belief that somehow I'd prevail over an uncertain future. It was possible, in that moment, to believe her.

When I got back to the house, John had taken his old guys and Emmy for a nature walk according to the note he left pinned to the fridge. The house was quiet, a rarity. I made a cup of tea and took it to the window seat in the library where the sun streamed in at that time of day. I settled myself to do some serious thinking.

Here in Uncle Charles' old house, I'd found a contentment I never expected. I loved my work with the kids. I loved the way the sun lit up this window, the way the house seemed to welcome me back when I returned to it. I loved the old guys, loved their spirit, their manners, their gallantry to me. Even Guy treated me with respect. John said Guy wouldn't be with us much longer, that his care would soon require skilled nursing which we weren't equipped to handle. I'd miss him, although he was like a ghost now, moving silently in John's wake. Watching his old hand grope for John's brought tears to my eyes sometimes.

Even though we lived in the same house, I couldn't figure John out. I'd never met a more caring person, but something was lacking. Humility is a wonderful trait, but it can be taken to extremes. I wondered again what his upbringing must have been like. He'd told me about his disengaged parents and a close relationship with an elderly neighbor. It explained part of what made him tick. Then his terrible prison experience and branding as a pedophile in the eyes of the law had convinced him he was forever unworthy. Yet I knew no one more worthy of having a good life. I knew he wanted to have that good life with me, but I just didn't have those feelings about him. Was I being unfair in living here so happily with him, keeping him hoping?

Billy was my first love, but that love was long gone by the time he'd come home on that first leave, riding his high horse, trying to tell me how to raise my daughter. His daughter, too, to be fair. But still, he had no right.

Now he was different, vulnerable and wounded. His injuries had forced him to pause in his clawing upward climb. I hoped he'd take time to reevaluate his life. I couldn't predict what the future held for him, but it would be happening to a man I didn't really know. The boy I'd loved was gone. Still, Billy was Emmy's father. Did I owe her a life with two parents? I didn't want to leave Grand Butte, my mom and dad, my day-care kids, this house. Decisions would have to be made, though.

I heard voices, the door opening, and Emmy's high-pitched chatter. They were back, and my moment of introspection was over. Relieved to put it aside, I moved to join the group in the kitchen. I'd think about it again later.

I was becoming increasingly worried about Guy. His combative stage had passed, but he no longer recognized his daughter-in-law, even though Marcie Willett visited him several times a week. Of even more concern was his tendency to choke on his food. Alzheimer's patients lose the ability to swallow; it's one of the final stages of their personal hell. Guy was almost there. I was thickening his water with a little corn starch and feeding him soft foods, but he still had episodes of pop-eyed, red-faced choking. It scared the kids, who would cluster around patting his back while he regained his breath.

He clung to me like a silent shadow, clutching my hand, holding onto my shirt if my hands were busy. It drove me nuts, but I tolerated it because I knew it gave him a little comfort. At night, he didn't venture past the "dark hole" throw rug in front of his door, but he'd cry out at all hours. Like a parent, I was attuned to his voice, so I always woke up, consequently spending most days in a haze of exhaustion. It was like having a needy infant without the cuteness factor. I asked Dr. Martin to drop by for a consultation. It was too hard to take Guy to the doctor's office.

The doc looked as tired as I did. He spent some time with Guy, did a physical examination and talked to him. Then he and I sat at the kitchen table with cups of coffee. We both needed the caffeine.

"You know it's time for Guy to be admitted into care," Dr. Martin said, wearily passing his hand over his face. "He's getting down to the wire with this god-awful disease. With the best will in the world, you can't give him the care he needs here."

"I just hate to move him," I said. "He'll be totally lost in a new place, with new people."

"That becomes less and less of a factor," Dr. Martin said. "He's attached to you because apparently there's some trace of memory that tells him he knows you and you'll keep him safe, but that will soon be gone. Then everyone will be equally a stranger to him, and every place will be new every day. And soon he'll be past that, too, until merciful death comes for him."

"Do you ever get used to it?" I asked.

"No. It breaks my heart every time. I've known the Willetts since I hung out my shingle. They were among my first patients and will be among my last, I guess."

"What's wrong, Doc?" I asked gently. "I can see you're not well yourself."

"Ah, John, you've got a good eye." He looked out the window for a long moment before he spoke again. "I have cancer, Stage Four. I've got maybe a year. That's not for public consumption yet. I'm trying to find someone to take over my practice before I tell folks I'm retiring. Don't want to leave them high and dry. But it's damn difficult to find a doctor who wants to live in a remote mountain town, miles from the latest technology and modern hospitals. I've been asking around, but the only nibble was from an older physician looking to coast into retirement in a scenic spot. I want a young, vigorous practitioner who will become part of Grand Butte for years."

There it was again, that devotion to a place and community, even in the face of personal trial. Grand Butte citizens seemed to drink it in their water. I sat in silence for a few minutes, turning over this new development in my mind.

"Doc, I'm so sorry," I said. "What can I do to help?"

"Find me a replacement," Dr. Martin said with a rueful smile.

I paused to gather my thoughts. Then I said, "What if there was a good doctor who wanted a small town practice? A guy comfortable with a hands-on approach, rather than relying on technology for every diagnosis."

"Do you know somebody like that?" Dr. Martin asked.

"I might. Let me make a phone call and get back to you."

Of course, I was thinking of Papa Doc. I hadn't been in touch with him since I'd left prison, but it hadn't been that long ago. He was probably still there. I went out to my car and rooted through the papers in my glove compartment. There it was: the phone number he'd scrawled on the back of an envelope. "Just in case you ever need me," he'd said, flashing his bright, white smile at me.

I went back inside and dialed, expecting to leave a voice mail message on the prison exchange. Instead, a familiar lilting voice answered. He'd given me his personal cell number.

"Doc, it's me, John. John Carver," I said.

"John! It's good to hear from you, mon. Where are you? What are you up to?"

"It's a long story, and I'll tell it to you in every detail, but first let me ask you a question. Would you be interested in looking at a medical practice that's for sale? It's in a remote mountain village, not a lot of bells and whistles but really nice people and pretty scenery."

I felt I'd put it too baldly. There was a long pause, then Papa Doc said, "Now let me get this right, John. You are telling me you know of a doctor looking for a replacement – not a locum tenens, but a buyer for his practice. Is it in the place where you live now?"

"Yes, I live in Grand Butte. It's a small place with only one doctor and he treats everything."

"How are the schools?" Papa Doc asked.

"Schools? You mean, grade and high school?"

"Yes. I have a family, John. Two little boys who must have good educations. That would be a primary consideration in any move my wife and I would make."

"I have to admit I don't know," I said. "There's probably a lot I don't know about what would be important to you. But listen: why don't you come and visit, find out for yourself? Bring your family. Meet the guy who's retiring, look at available housing. Get a feel for the place. You can stay with me."

"You've got a house then, John?"

"Well, yeah, that's a long story, too. But there's plenty of room and you'd be comfortable."

"Let me talk it over with Elise," Papa Doc said. "May I call you back tomorrow with my answer?"

I said that would be fine and gave him a rough idea of the route he'd take if they visited. We hung up and I called Dr. Martin.

"Have I got a doc for you!"

The Cambrones looked as exotic and beautiful as tropical birds, attracting much interest as they strolled Grand Butte's main street. Dr. Martin walked beside them, introducing them to everyone as friends who'd dropped by for a visit. They went by the elementary school, chatting with the principal who was alone in his office, working in his shirt sleeves during summer break. They toured Dr. Martin's office space, Etienne peppering Dr. Martin with questions about his case load, reimbursement, office staffing and what he did with patients who needed hospitalization.

"We have a couple of first-rate paramedics in the volunteer fire department who staff our only ambulance," he said. "If someone needs to go to the hospital, those guys take them. We haven't lost a patient yet."

Bree took the Cambrone boys into her play-group without batting an eyelash. The other kids asked a lot of questions about their inky black skin, patted their tight curls, and then everyone went back to constructing an elaborate city in the sandbox.

Dr. Martin drove Etienne and Elise around town so they could look at houses for sale. She was thrilled with one particular house, a Craftsman bungalow at least fifty years old. Dr. Martin called the realtor so the Cambrones could see the inside. That made the town's collective antenna go up: were these strangers thinking of settling in Grand Butte? If so, why? Dr. Martin wouldn't be able to keep his secret for long.

When we all got back to the house, the sun was sinking behind the woods, Bree's kids had gone home to their parents and the Cambrone boys were quietly watching a video. The adults settled on the patio with tall drinks. Papa Doc was quiet, but his wife bubbled with enthusiasm.

"It would be the perfect place for us, Etienne, don't you

think?" she said. "The boys could walk to school from that wonderful little house, and you could walk to the office. No traffic, no steel bars and doors locking behind you. Nice people, not criminals."

"Now, Elise, people are people, even if they happen to be behind bars," Etienne said mildly.

"True, but some people are more apt to kill you," Elise replied, eyes flashing. "I would like to feel you are safe at work. I need to feel that."

Dr. Martin watched their exchange. "You'd certainly be safe in Grand Butte," he said, "but I don't want to sell you on this place. It's not for everyone, and whether it's for you is a decision you'll have to make."

"You should know I have not yet passed my boards. I am an internist but without portfolio, shall we say. I expect to pass when I take the test, but it has not happened yet. Does that make a difference in our discussions?" Etienne asked.

"I would expect you to become Board certified as quickly as possible," Dr. Martin said. "The people of Grand Butte deserve the finest care. I think you can deliver it, but you need the credentials."

"And I intend to get them," Etienne replied. "Elise and I must digest what we've seen and heard today," Etienne said. "May we sleep on it tonight and talk again in the morning?"

"Of course," Dr. Martin said, rising with a weary sigh he tried to stifle. "Take all the time you need."

I was the only other person who knew time was the one commodity Doc Martin was short on.

I was accustomed to being the first one up in the mornings, but on that next morning, I had company. Papa Doc had already started the coffee and was trying to master the intricacies of our old toaster. A smudge of black smoke told me he hadn't had much success.

"Here, let me do that," I said. "She's a cranky old beast; you have to know just how to coax her along."

He surrendered the job and poured us both a cup of coffee. We took our breakfasts out on the patio to watch the sun rise.

"Well, John," Papa Doc said, "this is a beautiful spot you've found for yourself. You promised me the long stories; I am ready to hear them."

I started at the beginning: my flight in a used car, rescuing Bree and Emmy, taking care of Charles, inheriting half the house, working as a respite care-giver for elderly men. When I paused for breath, Papa Doc was wide-eyed. He gestured for me to go on.

"Bree convinced me to let everyone know about my past," I said. "The folks kind of know me now. They actually took it pretty well, most of them. A lot better than I expected. I thought I'd have to keep moving if they found out."

"So it is known that you served time and that's where we met," he said. When I nodded, he said, "That's a relief. I would have hated to start my work in this place with a secret I had to keep."

"So you've decided? You're coming?" I asked.

"We are," he said. "We'll see if we can rent the house Elise likes and I will join Dr. Martin for as long as he can continue working. When he decides to step down, I will buy his practice. If it all goes well, as I hope and believe," he added cautiously.

"That's great, Papa Doc! I couldn't be happier. I think you'll love it here."

"One thing, though, John," he said, eyeing me sternly.

"Sure, anything."

"Papa Doc stays behind in prison. Here I'm just your friend, Etienne."

# Chapter Ten

When I heard that about John, I saw red, I did, and understood for the first time what that old saying meant. It was Dad who told me. We were sitting on the porch after supper while Mom washed the dishes. Usually Dad doesn't say much, but I could tell he had something on his mind that evening. He cleared his throat a couple of times and finally said, "You don't want to get too mixed up with those folks in Charles' old house."

"Yeah? Why's that? My daughter is one of those folks."

"Well, there's something you don't know," Dad said.

"So tell me."

Dad harrumphed a couple of times. Then he came out with it: "That John Carver, he's a child molester."

"No, Dad, you've got that wrong. No way. Not John. He's too timid, for one thing."

"Well, what kinda guy you think picks on children? John's been in prison for it, just got out before he came here," Dad said, looking out at the horizon.

"Where'd you get that?"

"It's all over town. He told Daw and Doc Martin. They said so."

That was a different matter. If the two most respected men in town said so, it was so. I felt a cold chill run up my spine.

"I can't believe Bree would allow someone like that around Emmy," I said.

"Well, you don't know her as well as you think, then," Dad said. "She ain't the girl you used to run around with. Biggity now, going to inherit that house and probably a bunch of cash. At the end of the year, I reckon she'll buy him out and he'll be on his way. Guess Bree'd do anything for that, even put her own kid in danger."

"Emmy's my kid, too!" I said. My head felt like it would explode. That awful booming sound was back, the feeling of danger all around me, the fury of being helpless to make it stop. I didn't realize I'd leaped to my feet until I felt my fists pounding the porch railing. Dad was looking at me with something like fear in his eyes. I didn't care. I reached around the screen door and lifted his truck keys from the hook inside the door.

"Hey, now, son, you can't just take my truck..."

But I could and I did, screeching out of the driveway so fast it made the old truck rock. I couldn't get to Bree's place fast enough.

When I got close to the house, though, I pulled over beside the road. I'd had time to calm down a little bit and think what I was going to do. I had to get Emmy out of there. I had to focus. She wasn't safe, and as her father, it was up to me to make her safe. But I knew I couldn't just go roaring in and grab her. Bree would never let that happen. I'd have to be smart. I thought back to my Army recon days.

We'd approach the target by stealth, scout the perimeter, figure out where all the entrances and exits were, and the fastest escape route. We'd know how many people were there, what they were doing and if they were armed. Assess the threat, I told myself. I slipped into the woods and approached the house on foot, cloaked in the gathering dusk.

Lights glowed in the windows and cast bright paths on the shadowy lawn. I stayed in the shadows and slithered up beside a window. It was the one over the kitchen sink and it was open. I could hear laughter and conversation as they ate supper around the pine kitchen table. I made out Emmy's voice as she chattered unintelligibly. Bree and John could understand everything she said, but I could only pick up a word here and there. The old guys were yakking about some sports thing they were going to watch on television that night. I risked a peek. John's chair was pushed back and he was bouncing Emmy on his foot while she squealed, "Horsey! Horsey!" That one old guy, the crazy one, was hanging onto John's sleeve. I felt the red veil descending over my sight again. There he sat like King Tut, surrounded by admirers. Dirty pervert, there he sat, like it didn't even matter.

I longed for the feel of my M4 rifle in my hands. If I'd had that, it would have been all over for that little group of losers in the kitchen. Just grab my daughter and get the hell out of there. But that wasn't going to happen, so I had to be smart, make a plan. I crept around the house, looking in the windows of empty rooms lighted and waiting for their occupants. Bree's and Emmy's bedroom windows were open a few inches, letting in the fresh mountain breeze. A little lamp in Emmy's room outlined the white crib where she slept. I tested the screens; they were nylon mesh, not wire. Easy to cut. I felt for the knife I always carried in my pocket. Not yet. Not yet. I settled in for a long wait, but recon always involved waiting. I knew I could do it.

Emmy was tired and cranky. Bath time wasn't fun for either of us, but finally I had her clean and buttoned into her footie pajamas. "Rockaby?" I asked. Sometimes she wanted it, sometimes not. She shook her head no, eyes already at half-mast, thumb in mouth. I deposited her in her bed, wound up the blue kitty music box that played a lullaby, and tiptoed out of the room.

I'd wait a few minutes until she was good and asleep, then have a soak in the big tub in Charles' old master bathroom. John told me a funny story about his first experience getting Charles into that tub and I always smiled when I remembered it.

Life seemed good to me that night, I remember that. John was happy to have his old friend, Dr. Cambrone, coming to live in Grand Butte. I liked Elise Cambrone and looked forward to getting to know her better. Doc Martin was clearly relieved at the prospect of having help with the daily grind of private practice. So I soaked happily in a deep bath full of bubbles, feeling no foreboding.

It's never the things you worry about that actually happen; it's the stuff that whistles up out of left field and whacks you on the head when you're not looking. I never expected that, when I went to check on Emmy later than evening, her crib would be empty.

~*~

She was sleeping soundly when I picked her up. I thought maybe she'd wake, but she didn't even stir when her thumb fell out of her mouth. I carried her carefully over to the now wide-open window, stuck a leg through and then the other. My spine stabbed with pain as I hit the ground. Good thing her bedroom was on the ground floor. We were out of the house. My baby was safe with me. I started walking toward

Dad's truck. I wasn't sure where I'd go, but I figured I'd just drive. With any luck, Bree wouldn't discover Emmy was gone until morning. We'd be far away by then. A thought was buzzing around at the edges of my mind, but I was too full of adrenalin to capture it. That rush kept my legs pumping until we reached the truck.

But wait! There were lights and people there. I heard my Dad's voice. He'd figured out where I was heading and had come after me, Mom driving him in her old car. Now they intended to take the truck and let me make my way home as best I could. Teach the boy a lesson. I knew how they thought.

I'd pocketed the truck key, but Mom apparently had a spare. Right now, they were fussing about getting it off of her key ring. They both had their heads down in the glare of Mom's headlights.

"I can't get the dang ring apart," Dad was saying. "Here, you got fingernails, you pry it off."

They didn't see or hear me. I stepped quietly into the woods that grew right up to the road. My head buzzed. Okay, no truck. I was a trained Army soldier. I could manage just fine in the dark forest. The only thing that mattered was keeping Emmy safe. I'd figure it out as I went along.

She was dead weight in my arms, her head cradled on my shoulder. It was the first time I'd held my daughter like that. She smelled of shampoo and clean clothes. Her silky hair tickled my cheek. I loved her so much in that moment, so much I knew I'd do anything to keep her safe.

How are you going to do that? You don't know anything about babies. You don't know how to take care of your own kid. You're in the woods in the middle of the night. What if she wakes up? What if she cries? What if she's scared?

My legs were numb. My spine wasn't healed enough for me

to walk on uneven ground carrying even Emmy's light weight. I put one foot in front of the other, never quite sure where it would land. If only that terrible noise, that booming in my head, would stop. Then I could think, figure out what to do next.

~*~

Bree's scream sucked all the air out of the house. I jumped from my chair where I'd been dozing in front of the television and ran toward her voice.

"She's gone, she's gone, oh my god, John, she's gone!"

Emmy's crib was empty, the window gaped open and the cut screen fluttered in the breeze. Bree was halfway out of the window when I grabbed her and pulled her back inside. She fought me, but I hung on until she stopped.

"Okay, okay, Bree, we'll find her, but we have to use our heads now, not just run off in the dark. Somebody took her, but we'll find her."

"It was Billy," Bree said flatly. "I know it was him."

"What makes you think that?" I asked, walking her into the kitchen, reaching for the phone.

"I just know. I'm her mother, I know," Bree said. "I've seen the way he looks at her. He thinks he'd be a better parent than I am. He wants to take her from me. I'll kill him first, John, I mean it."

Etienne came into the kitchen. "What's going on?" he asked. "We heard screaming."

I explained as briefly as possible, and he nodded. "Elise will stay here with Guy and the kids. I will come with you to search," he said, as always quick to grasp the situation and waste no words.

I dialed Daw's number. He was there within minutes and

shortly after came a number of men and boys. Their pick-up trucks lined the gravel driveway. Daw had a strong light which he trained on the ground under Emmy's window. We saw a crumpled baseball hat and footprints in the dew-wet grass. Bree grabbed the hat out of Daw's hands just as he was about to slip it into a plastic evidence bag.

"I need this," she said. "It's Billy's." Daw studied her face, shrugged and let her have it.

A deputy photographed the area, then instructed two of the men to loop yellow crime-scene tape around it to keep it undisturbed until he had time to make plaster casts of the prints. Somehow, seeing that yellow tape, such a television cliché, made it seem terribly real.

Bree was gulping air as if there wasn't enough to fill her lungs. She'd changed into her hiking boots and was carrying a big flashlight. This mother wouldn't be sitting tearfully in the house while men looked for her lost child. Her face was without color, set in lines of determination. She came over and linked her arm through mine.

"We're going to find her together," she said. "No one else knows her like we do, and no one knows Billy like I do. Come on."

We started for the woods, Etienne close behind, but then I stopped, held up one hand and ran back to the house. When I came out, I had Queenie on her leash beside me.

"She may not be a bloodhound, but she knows our girl," I said. "Find Emmy, Queenie. C'mon, let's go find Emmy."

Queenie looked at me with her head cocked to one side, clearly trying to figure out what she was supposed to do. Bree held out the cap and Queenie sniffed it. She looked at me again, then obediently trotted into the woods. I knew she still wasn't sure what we wanted of her, but she was a game little dog and she'd keep trying.

We entered the woods at the closest point from Emmy's window. Bree's flashlight constantly swept the ground in front of us. The spongy forest floor was carpeted with thick pine needles that showed no trace of footprints.

"He won't be able to get far, not with that back of his," Bree said.

We pressed on, calling Emmy's name and stopping every few minutes to listen for a response. The trees on this moonless night were tall shadows, somehow menacing. Around us, we heard other searchers crashing through underbrush, voices echoing the call "Emmy, Emmy," into that black, indifferent forest. Bree's voice took on a ragged note. I could hear the tears behind it. I gripped her arm tighter.

I was making for the little hunting shack Dad built years ago. It was on Charles' land, but so deep in the forest not even Charles knew it was there. I wasn't sure if I could find it, it'd been so long, but if I could get there, I could put Emmy down and give my legs a rest.

Behind us, I heard the first signs of pursuit. Dammit! Bree must have discovered Emmy was missing already. I'd counted on having the night to get away. I ran and my jolting stride woke Emmy. She raised her head and looked at me, her eyes big with confusion I could sense even in the dark.

"Mama?" she said. Again, with a note of panic in her voice, "Mama?"

And then she was screaming. She had lungs, that kid. I panicked, fearing she could be heard all over the forest.

"Hush, Emmy!" I said. "Daddy's got you, now be quiet. We're going on an adventure, just you and Daddy."

"Mama!" Emmy wailed, beating at me with her little fists.

I stumbled and fell to my knees. Getting back on my feet was almost impossible with Emmy frantically hitting and kicking, but I did it. The roaring in my ears made it really hard to think. I shook Emmy just a little to make her stop that damned yelling. You'll get us caught. Shut up; shut up. I put my hand over her mouth and she bit me with her sharp baby teeth. I shook her again, a little harder, and kept my hand tight over her mouth. Maybe her nose, too. It was too dark to see. She went limp.

That made her easier to carry, but I was scared. What had I done? I stopped and put her down on the forest floor. She was so tiny, so still. Maybe she'd gone back to sleep. I found I couldn't pick her up and still rise to my feet. Legs just wouldn't work. So I stretched out beside her and closed my eyes. Maybe we'd rest a while. Just sleep a little.

But then I heard Bree's voice: "Emmy! Emmy!" Emmy didn't stir, but I scrambled up somehow, grabbing onto a tree. Where was Bree? Could she see me? She'd been so nice to me earlier, but now she'd be mad that I took Emmy. But I was mad too. How could Bree put Emmy in danger by living with that creep? My hands tingled with the desire to put them around Bree's neck and squeeze and squeeze, to hit John's face and feel his bones break. It was her fault, all of this was her fault. I was just trying to rescue my daughter, my little girl. But then my anger faded, replaced by a sinking feeling that I'd done something terribly wrong. I couldn't sort it out.

Emmy was sleeping now, safely away from John; I'd come back for her when everybody gave up the search and went home. I stooped and heaped some leaves over her to keep her warm. Then I ran as best I could. My feet didn't seem to work and I knew I must be plowing a trail through the forest floor. I no longer had a destination, except away. In my head drummed the Army injunction, leave no man behind; leave no man behind. Yet I was leaving my little daughter behind. Was I any better than John? I held my head in my hands as I stumbled along, trying to contain the sound that had become an all-encompassing roar.

We walked and ran and fell down and got back up and ran some more. How could Billy have gotten this far on his bad legs, with that bad back? My voice was gone, I could only croak out Emmy's name. Fear washed over me in great waves. If John hadn't been supporting me I'd have fallen to the ground. We'd stop every few steps to listen, hoping to hear her cry, but all we heard were the other searchers crashing through the forest, calling her name.

Queenie seemed to be as dazed and disoriented as I felt. She was just a house-dog, a pet, not a tracker. She was familiar with the woods, but she'd never been out in them in the middle of the night any more than I had. It was stupid of John to bring her, she only slowed us down. Besides, she wasn't cooperating; she kept pulling on John's arm to go in the opposite direction.

"Wait up, Bree," John said.

I stopped, barely able to contain my compulsion to keep moving. "Let's just stop and think a minute," John said. "We're assuming Billy took Emmy and went straight into the woods. What if he didn't? What if he walked along the road? We may be looking in the wrong place. Queenie wants to go back towards the road."

"Queenie!" I said derisively. She pricked her ears and looked at me. "What the hell does Queenie know?"

"What the hell do we know, Bree? We're running blind here. Queenie can smell scents we can't even imagine. Let's pay attention to her."

Etienne nodded. He'd been our silent companion, his eyes constantly scanning the forest around us in the path of his flashlight. "I agree," he said. "I've seen no broken branches or trampled vegetation that would have marked a man's passage. I think we are looking in the wrong place."

So we turned and followed Queenie. She tugged on the leash, wanting to run, and we picked up the pace with her. Somehow her excitement was contagious and I felt a surge of hope. She led us to the road, nose to the ground, and we walked along it for maybe a quarter of a mile. Then she turned and darted into the woods.

There was definitely a trail for us to follow. Our eyes had become accustomed to the dark, and now I could see that twigs and branches were bent and the pine straw underfoot was scuffled. I called Emmy's name as best I could, but my voice was too weak to carry far. John called, too, and when we stopped to listen, we heard a rustling ahead of us. We ran towards it. The moon chose that moment to emerge from behind the low clouds where it had been hiding, and in that blue illumination I saw Billy. He was crouching over something on the ground, jabbering to himself, rocking back and forth. He didn't seem to notice us as we approached him. Etienne held out one hand to stop us and stepped ahead.

"Billy," he said softly, "I'm a doctor and I've come to help you with Emmy. Where is she, Billy? Can you show me?"

"Leave no man behind. Leave no man behind. Leave no man behind," Billy chanted, continuing his rocking.

I saw a little mound beside him and John saw it too. He held back my scream with his hand. Etienne approached Billy slowly.

"Is that her, there on the ground?" he asked.

Billy didn't answer.

"May I take a look, make sure she's okay?" Etienne asked.

Billy looked up then. "She's sleeping," he said. "I covered her with leaves so she wouldn't get cold."

"Good, that was good thinking; you're taking care of her," Etienne said, his voice low and even. "I'll just brush these leaves off her face."

"No! Don't wake her!" Billy said. He knelt over Emmy, the moonlight flashing on the knife that suddenly appeared in his hand. "You stay back. I'm protecting her."

"Protecting her from what?" Etienne asked.

"From that dirty pervert, from John," Billy said.

I felt John tense beside me. Now I held him back.

"You are a good father," Etienne said, "That's what good fathers do, isn't it? We protect our children. Let me help you protect her. Here, give me the knife." He held out his palm.

Billy hesitated, then handed it over, scooting backward on his heels with a weary sigh. Etienne knelt beside the little mound that was my daughter. Gently he brushed the leaves from her face, then from her chest. He bent low to put his ear on her heart, experienced fingers pressing on her carotid artery. I held my breath and prayed with everything that was in me.

"She's breathing," he said, loud enough for us to hear, but careful not to look in our direction. Billy was still unaware of our presence. Etienne felt Emmy's neck carefully. Then he rubbed two fingers up and down her sternum. Nothing. He tapped on her collarbone.

She stirred! I saw her move and my being was flooded with a relief so intense I sagged to the ground. John let me slide. He never took his eyes off of Billy.

"I'm going to take Emmy to her mama," Etienne said softly.

"That's okay, isn't it, Billy? The baby should be with her mama, yes?"

Billy nodded, his head in his hands. Etienne picked up Emmy, who was beginning to whimper, and walked to where I was standing. She reached out her arms for me and I pressed her to my heart. Etienne put his arm around my shoulders, turning me for the careful walk back home. Behind us, I heard John speak.

"Billy, look at me," he said in a voice I'd never heard before.

I looked over my shoulder and saw him standing over Billy, who was still sitting on the ground.

"I'm not what you said. I'm not a child molester or a pervert. You got it wrong. You'll never call me that again, you understand?"

Billy raised his head and blinked up at John. "But my dad said...."

"I don't care what your dad said; now you're hearing from me. I will not carry that poisonous label for something I didn't do. I know you've got your own troubles, and maybe you're not thinking clearly right now. But it's important that you understand me. I would never hurt Emmy or any child."

Billy nodded once. He dropped his head back into his hands. John left him there on the forest floor and hurried to catch up with us.

At the house, Etienne put Emmy on the kitchen table and went over her little body thoroughly, shining his flashlight in her eyes, palpating her belly and feeling along the length of every limb. She seemed sleepy and limp and when he was finished, he reached for the phone and dialed 911. He exchanged a meaningful look with John, who said, "Right. There's not room for all of us in the ambulance. Call me when you know."

Etienne rode with Emmy and me as we made our way down the winding roads to the nearest hospital. The keening siren took me back to another emergency ride we'd taken down the mountain. Surely my daughter wasn't spared in the car wreck only to be killed by her own father. We'd been okay then; surely, please God, we'd be okay now.

Emmy slept most of the way, but Etienne never took his fingers from her wrist. When we got there, he carried her into the emergency room himself. "I am Dr. Etienne Cambrone of Grand Butte. This two-year-old girl was found unconscious. I believe she has been shaken and smothered," he told the receiving physician. "My physical exam didn't show any overt signs of trauma, but she's lethargic. I want a scan to make sure there's no bleeding in her brain."

When Emmy was rolled away on an awfully big gurney for such a little girl, then for the first time I released the emotions I'd been holding back. I sank to the floor there in the ER corridor and cried until I ran out of tears.

We waited, Etienne and I, for an eternity before we heard that gurney returning. Emmy was sitting up, holding the hand of the nurse who walked beside her. It was the sweetest sight I'd ever seen.

The police received the hospital's report of an abused child. Five minutes before they showed up, there was Daw, on hand to greet his fellow lawmen and talk to them in their professional lingo. They listened respectfully, nodding and jotting in their narrow notebooks. There would be more legalities that I'd have to be a part of, but for tonight, Daw handled it. Once again, Grande Butte had wrapped its arms around me and my child.

We stayed in the hospital until morning, Emmy and I curled up together on the bed, Etienne asleep in the chair beside us. I didn't close my eyes; there was too much to savor. All my life, I'll remember Etienne's dear, tired face relaxed in sleep. I'll remember the beautiful scan that showed no brain damage. I'll remember the weight of Emmy's head on my shoulder, her wispy hair caressing my cheek. I'll remember John's tear-choked voice when I called with the good news. I'll remember every detail of that night, the night my daughter was lost and found.

# Chapter 11

Our year in Charles' house is up, but somehow neither of us has mentioned it. I keep waiting for Bree to bring it up; maybe she's waiting for me. We're so busy that sometimes a full day passes without our exchanging more than a couple of words.

Our home-based enterprises are flourishing. Bree has eight children in her play-group, plus Emmy. She found she needed help, and Rosita decided to quit her job at the diner and join Bree full-time. Bree can't afford to pay her much, but Rosita gets to be with her kids all day.

I talk to the parents before they leave their child in our house, tell them what happened to me and invite them to ask all the questions they want. So far, no one has turned away. They tell me they feel lucky to have such great day-care at such a good price. I hear the same thing from the families of my adult charges.

"John's old guys," as they call themselves, number four right now, although I've had up to six at one time. They come to me for different reasons -- socialization, care while they recuperate from various illnesses or operations, or maybe because their worlds are getting fuzzy and unpredictable and they're scared. Some stay for a little while, some become regulars. Etienne stops by and checks on them to make sure we don't miss any symptoms we could handle proactively.

Guy went to a nursing home, where he died after a four-month stay. Difficult as he could be, I still miss him. His daughter-in-law, Marcie, arrives for supper every Friday evening, carrying a covered dish to share. She says being around the other men helps her remember Guy at his best, not as he was in those last years.

Carl remains with us, our only permanent resident and in-house grandpa. He still speaks with grateful wonder about how he never expected his life to include children. Most days he can be found helping with the kids, reading to a circle of intent little faces, or rocking a fussy baby. Carl is aging backwards. He seems younger now than when he came to us.

The Cambrones have lived in Grand Butte for six months. They are our closest friends. Bree, especially, will cherish Etienne forever for his help with Emmy on that awful night.

Etienne had to overcome a bit of resistance when he appeared in Dr. Martin's practice. There aren't many black families in Grand Butte, and while there was no overt prejudice, there was a bit of wariness. Some patients, for instance, asked for the "real doctor," but Etienne took it in stride. His big smile and genuine concern for his patients soon won over even the most reluctant. Dr. Martin is giving up both his practice and his life gradually and gracefully. I hope I will have the same serenity when my time comes.

We don't often talk about the night Billy took Emmy. It was such a huge experience for all of us. I guess we're still trying to process it. Emmy herself doesn't remember anything, at least not consciously. She's made a full recovery physically, but she clings to her mama at bedtime. I've seen Bree sitting beside her crib many nights, her head bowed over her daughter, holding one little hand.

Billy is in a VA hospital. Daw took him there himself, and stayed until Billy got checked in and settled in his room. Post-Traumatic Stress Disorder, of course. It doesn't take a genius to figure that out. People are sympathetic, despite the terrible thing he did. If he gets his life together, he'll be welcome back in his home town. But somehow, I don't think he'll ever live here again.

His parents still keep to themselves, which is a shame because they're missing an adorable grandchild. Bree, usually so generous with forgiveness, has not forgiven them. She believes they nearly cost Emmy her life. Billy, she can understand and almost pardon; he's battling his own demons. But his parents, particularly his father, did damage out of willful ignorance and spite. That's what she finds unforgiveable.

I'm still in love with Bree, now more than ever. Time has only deepened it. I'd do anything for her, including leave if it would make her happy. But if it never works out with her, if she never comes to love me, then I'll deal with it. The worst thing that could happen would be losing her as my best friend. I don't pester her with my feelings, but I think she knows.

John is different. He seems taller, although I guess he was always a couple of inches taller than I, and he walks with the confidence of a man who owns his space. He looks people straight in the eye. No more secrets. That night in the forest was the turning point for him. He never talks about leaving anymore. The humiliated boy is gone, and in his place stands a man. I liked the boy. I respect the man.

I know John's waiting for me to say something about our year in Charles' house being up. We're free to move on now, but the life we've built here is so satisfying that I want it to continue. I love working with my kids; I love the house and living in it with John and Carl and little Queenie, who is now truly Queen of Everything because she found my baby girl. John made me stop cooking special treats for her when she began to get fat.

Sometimes I think it would be great to have a sibling for Emmy. It would be wonderful to be someone's beloved, to be the light in someone's eyes. Well, honestly, I already am. John doesn't speak of it, but he docsn't have to.

It's not the right time for me just now. I'm still young, and my past mistakes have made me cautious. Before I take on a relationship, I want to be confident I'm really a grown-up, like John is. He came into my life a perfect stranger and now I can't imagine living without him. I wonder what it would be like to be married to my best friend.

He's jingling the car keys at me, signaling me to quit day-dreaming over my shopping list and get going. We have errands to run in town. Driving down the twisting mountain road, we come to the scene of my wreck. John parks the car on the spot where it happened, and we sit for a moment in silence. He reaches over and runs his thumb over the fading scar on my forehead. Then he takes my hand. I feel a little tingle when our hands touch. This time, I take his face in my hands and kiss him. When we part, his eyes are full of questions; he doesn't speak, just pulls me close. I rest my head on his shoulder.

"John, there's something I've been wanting to ask you," I say.

"What?"

"Would you call me by my real name? Would you call me Brenna?"

Marcie Willett talked to the principal of the high school before she talked to me. When she approached me with her idea, she said with a nervous giggle that it was all arranged, and I couldn't say no. "I want you to talk to the high school kids about your experience," she said.

When I opened my mouth to protest, she held out her hand like a traffic cop. "Don't say anything right away," she said. "Hear me out. I believe you have something very valuable to share with those kids – real-world experience coming from a guy not that much older than they are. Wouldn't you love to prevent them from going through what you went through? Wouldn't it validate your suffering if you could?"

"Sure. But my gosh, it's very personal," I said. "I'm not sure I could stand in front of an audience and pretend I've overcome it. In many ways, I haven't."

"But in many other ways, you have," Marcie insisted. "And anyway, there's a lot of value in a cautionary tale." She grinned at me and I couldn't help grinning back.

"Let me think about it," I said.

That's how I came to be standing on the stage in the high school auditorium, looking out over a sea of young faces, feeling the wings of frenzied butterflies beating in my stomach. The principal finished his introduction, of which I heard nothing, and turned to me with a smile. I rose from my chair, stood behind the podium and straightened my spine. Bree smiled from the back row, giving me a shot of confidence.

"Hi, everybody," I said. "My name is John Carver and when I was eighteen, I went to prison for statutory rape. Let me tell you what happened."

~End~

# About the Author

Doris Reidy began her writing career in third grade, when a poem about fairies dancing in the moonlight was published in the local newspaper. (Hindsight suggests it was a slow news day.) In later years, she wrote non-fiction articles for *Redbook*, *Writer's Digest* and *Atlanta Magazine*, among others, and a monthly book review column for the *Atlanta Journal* and *Constitution*. Then came a long silence during which life intervened, followed by a second act as a novelist. ***Imperfect Stranger*** is her fourth novel.

Please follow Doris Reidy on Facebook and **dorisreidy.com**, and leave your feedback at **reidybooks@gmail.com**.

## Turn the page for a special bonus...

Prepare to sit back, relax, and enjoy a tale from Doris Reidy's hilarious collection of short stories about the implacable, one-of-a-kind Mrs. Entwhistle. The entire volume of stories about her is available now.

# Mrs. Entwhistle Attends Her
# High School Reunion

"Did you get your invitation?" Maxine asked. She was waving hers in the air.

"Yes, I got it," Mrs. Entwhistle said dismissively. "But I'm not going. It just wouldn't be the same without Floyd."

"Now, Cora, you've been saying that every year since Floyd passed. Let's just go this year. We'll whisper about how old everyone else looks." Maxine's eyes danced with the fun of conspiracy, but Mrs. Entwhistle was unmoved.

"No, I don't think so," she said. "Floyd loved it, and I only went because of him. High school reunions aren't my cup of tea. Just a lot of disappointingly old folks trying to remember their glory days. And the only people who show up are the ones, like us, who stayed in town. You know it'll be the same people we see at the grocery store and church and the library. It might be more interesting if some of those who moved off would come back."

"Well, then!" Maxine said delightedly. "There's no excuse for you not to go this year, because guess who's going to be there!"

"Who?"

"Giancarlo Cicerino."

Maxine sat back to enjoy the look of amazement on Mrs. Entwhistle's face.

"Really?"

"That's what Mary Sue told me. He's coming all the way from California expressly for this reunion, because it's our sixtieth. Mary Sue said when Giancarlo called her to make his reservation, he said anybody who is still standing is someone he wants to see."

Giancarlo had been the shining star of their high school days. He played football, had his own convertible, was class president, and dated Janine Hasselfress, the prettiest girl in school. Mrs. Entwhistle'd had a secret crush on him for most of senior year, but she'd never breathed a word of it, not even to Maxine. With his smoldering dark Italian eyes and black hair, Giancarlo was out of her league. Besides, she was already going out with Floyd. She suspected Floyd had an inkling of how she felt, though. He'd never liked Giancarlo. Called him Sissy-Pants Cicerino.

"Well. Maybe. It would be fun to see how Giancarlo has aged. Living out there in all that sunshine, he might have the hide of a walrus by now."

"I bet he doesn't," Maxine said dreamily. "I bet he doesn't."

She reached into her capacious bag and pulled out an ancient yearbook. Mrs. Entwhistle couldn't believe Max had not only kept it all these years, but could put her hands on it when she wanted to. Together they scanned the formal black and white graduation photographs of their fellow classmates. Under each picture was a Senior Superlative that supposedly summed up character. Mrs. Entwhistle had been on the yearbook committee and remembered how they'd pondered these descriptors. There was Floyd Entwhistle – Most Industrious; herself, Cora Johnson – Most Determined; Maxine Gober – Best Friend. And Giancarlo Cicerino, smiling confidently into his bright future – Most Likely to Succeed. Privately, Mrs. Entwhistle agreed with Maxine. She bet Giancarlo didn't look like a walrus, either.

~*~

Mrs. Entwhistle hadn't worried about what to wear in a long time. She had her pantsuit, old but still good, that she wore for special occasions, and a couple of nice church dresses. Surveying them in her closet gave her no pleasure. The pantsuit had big shoulder-pads; she was pretty sure they were no longer in style. But if she wore one of the dresses, that meant she'd have to wear pantyhose. Ronnie Sue said nobody but old ladies wore pantyhose anymore. The fact that Mrs. Entwhistle was an old lady did not make her amenable to joining their fashion ranks. She'd noticed that young women just stuffed their naked feet into high heels and went bare-legged. That was all very well if you had smooth, brown legs. Mrs. Entwhistle did not.

"Maxine, I think maybe I'll buy a new outfit," she said one day, trying to sound off-hand. "Not just for the reunion, of course. Something I could wear any time."

"Why, yes, Cora, you should. I saw a beautiful white pantsuit in Kresyln's window."

"No, I'd look like a nurse in all white. Heaven knows, nurses will probably be needed at our class reunion, but I don't want to be mistaken for one."

"Do you want to go out to the mall? I'll drive, if you want to go."

The mall was a major undertaking for the two ladies. It squatted beside the frightening interstate. Mrs. Entwhistle had given up driving in those snorting, whirling, eddying, horn-blasting, whooshing lanes, but Maxine still ventured forth in her big Lincoln. Mrs. Entwhistle thought Maxine wasn't scared only because she couldn't see or hear very well. She sat so low she had to peek over the top of the steering wheel. Mrs. Entwhistle, taller, saw the near-misses and heard the angry horn-blasts. It was terrifying. But desperate times call for desperate measures.

Mrs. Entwhistle said, "Well, okay, then."

~*~

The ladies emerged from the Lincoln's front seat a little flustered. They fluffed their hair, clutched their purses firmly, took deep breathes and launched themselves into the perfume-scented, Muzak-filled mall. They headed to Macy's, a store with which they were long familiar. But it had been a year since their last visit and everything seemed to have been moved. They wandered for a few minutes, but Mrs. Entwhistle knew they had neither the stamina nor the feet to wander long. She approached a sales clerk at the cosmetics counter, got sprayed with perfume for her trouble, but learned the way to Women's.

Once there, they scanned the racks and racks of spring clothing. "Everything's sleeveless," Maxine said sadly.

"And short," Mrs. Entwhistle added. "Let's ask where the Alfred Dunner section is."

That was more like it. There were plenty of elastic waistbands and elbow-length sleeves, styles they favored. Mrs. Entwhistle picked out a pantsuit in basic black and held it out for Maxine's inspection. But Max was holding out something herself: a long, periwinkle blue dress. Mrs. Entwhistle shook her head no.

"Oh, try it on, Cora," Maxine said. "This color would be lovely on you."

"But a long dress, Max? I mean, we're just going to be in the school cafeteria."

"You didn't read your invitation very carefully," Maxine said. "The reunion is in the Marriott, the one on the south side of town. It's going to be fancy this year. And besides, long dresses are in style, even for daytime. I'll wear one if you will. Just slip it on. I think it will be perfect for you."

And it was. Mrs. Entwhistle's critical self-assessing eyes raked her image up and down in the full-length, three-way mirror, and she had to admit she looked good. Pretty good. For seventy-eight. Well, that's all you could reasonably expect, right? The long sweep of blue reminded her of how tall and slim she'd been when she was young.

"I'll take it," Mrs. Entwhistle said. "I'll get my hair done at the Curl-E-Cue Corner and wear my pearl earrings." She felt a frisson of excitement.

Shoes. High heels were out of the question. "Don't need a broken hip," Mrs. Entwhistle said. She tried on a pair of silver slippers. They had absolutely no arch-support and she knew her legs would ache for days after wearing them, but somehow they made her rather large, rather flat feet look smaller. Almost dainty. She bought them. Then she bought a tiny silver beaded purse on a chain.

"Do you think I'd have time to lose a few pounds?" Mrs. Entwhistle had the bit in her teeth now.

"Oh, Cora, why torment yourself?" Maxine said. "You look fine just as you are. Besides, if you lost weight, you'd lose it all in the face. Remember Jenny?"

They had a mutual friend who'd bragged incessantly about losing twenty pounds, seemingly unaware that, as a result, her face had melted into a million wrinkles. The memory made the corners of their mouths turned up just a little bit. Better to keep the plump cheeks, and put up with the other plump parts.

Mrs. Entwhistle declared herself ready. Now she had only to wait. How ridiculous to feel nervous little butterflies in her stomach. For heaven's sake. At her age. And for Sissy-Pants Ciserino. Floyd would have a fit.

~*~

The Marriott's ballroom was too big for their little gathering. Only about fifty people milled around the bar, and maybe half of them were spouses. You could tell the spouses by their bored faces. Nothing worse than somebody else's class reunion, Mrs. Entwhistle thought. She and Floyd had graduated together, so they both knew everyone and shared the memories of high-school high-jinks, so hilarious to those involved, so interminable to those not. You had to feel sorry for the poor husbands and wives of alumni, desperately making small talk and trying to hide glances at their watches.

It would have been impossible to identify the eighteen-year-olds now incarcerated in white heads and stooped bodies had each person not been wearing a name tag containing his or her graduation photo. Could this be bubbly Marilyn Dornan, this frail old lady? And James Keeler, he of the graceful jump shot, walking gingerly on traitorous knees? Frenchy Laurent, drum majorette, holding a cane instead of baton? But somehow, despite the extra pounds and wrinkles, they were laughing and talking, living up to their class motto, "Onward Ever, Backward Never." Mrs. Entwhistle felt a lump in her throat. They were all so brave.

Maxine was getting them both a Diet Coke and Mrs. Entwhistle stood alone by a column entwined with plastic ivy. She knew she must look as antiquated as everyone else, but curled and scented, powdered and lipsticked, wearing the long blue dress and silver slippers, she didn't even feel like herself. She'd worried about carrying her utilitarian black cane with her fancy clothes, but drew the line when Maxine suggested she get a flowered walking stick.

"For heaven's sake," she'd said. "All I need is some slippery new cane so I can fall flat on my face. No, I'll just stick with what I'm used to."

But she did hide it as best she could in the folds of her dress.

There was a stir over by the door. People were looking that way, drifting over, calling to each other. Mrs. Entwhistle looked, too, and saw the entrance of a short, rotund fellow. He was beaming, showing a lot of bright white teeth. His progress was slowed by hand-shaking, back-slapping and hugging, but as he drew nearer, Mrs. Entwhistle saw, with a thrill of recognition, that it was Giancarlo. Suddenly feeling shy, she shrank back behind the column.

Maxine, making her way across the room with a Diet Coke in each hand, was intercepted, thoroughly hugged and kissed on both cheeks by Giancarlo. Blushing a becoming pink, she reached Mrs. Entwhistle slightly out of breath.

"Whooee!" she said. "Here you go. Well, Giancarlo hasn't changed a bit, has he?"

"Was he always that short?" Mrs. Entwhistle said. "I remembered him as being much bigger."

"Well, I expect he's shrunk some," Max said. "But he wasn't ever a real big guy. He just acted like it."

"Is he here alone? No wife?"

"Looks that way. Here he comes now."

"Why, Cora Johnson, I'd know you anywhere!" Giancarlo said, eyeing her name tag as he grabbed Mrs. Entwhistle in a bear hug.

"It's Entwhistle," she gasped. "Oof!"

"Oh, so you married Floyd, then? I used to call him Fuddy-Duddy Floyd," Giancarlo said. "Where is that rascal?"

"He had a name for you, too," Mrs. Entwhistle said in an icy voice. Nobody, not even Giancarlo Cicerino, disparaged Floyd in her presence. "He passed several years ago."

"Oh, sorry to hear that. Great guy, great guy," Giancarlo said. "Let's sit together at dinner. We've got a lot to catch up on, am I right?"

Mrs. Entwhistle felt flattered in spite of herself, but the effect was somewhat spoiled when he turned and said exactly the same thing to Maxine. He offered each of them an arm, and escorted them to seats at one of the round tables.

"So!" Giancarlo said, beaming to his left and to his right. "How are you girls doing? Maxine, can you still fit into your cheerleader's outfit? And Cora, are you still the smartest girl in the room?"

"Well, I shouldn't think so," Mrs. Entwhistle said. "I've lived long enough to know how much I don't know. Besides, I've been in a lot of rooms since high school, haven't you?"

"Oh, yes, yes, indeed," said Giancarlo. If he'd had a mustache, he'd have twirled it. "Lived in California all these years, cradle of the movie industry, you know. My second wife, ex-wife, that is, was an actress. You may have heard of her – Myra McDonald?"

Mrs. Entwhistle and Maxine smiled and shook their heads.

"Well, she wasn't exactly famous, but she was in the

industry and we got to know a lot of people. That's what we call the movie business – the industry," he explained.

"What was your work?" Mrs. Entwhistle asked.

"I was in promotion, marketing, development, you know, ideas..." Giancarlo said, waving his hand vaguely. "I was an idea man."

"What exactly does an idea man do?" Mrs. Entwhistle wondered.

"We think up work for other people to do!" Giancarlo said, with a wink and a laugh. "Actually, I'm still at it."

Mrs. Entwhistle thought of the years in which Floyd rose at six a.m., made a pot of coffee and brought her a cup, then set off for a full day's work at the airplane factory. When he retired, he got a plaque and a camera to take pictures of all the trips they never had time to take before he died. Floyd didn't expect other people to do work he thought up for them. He did it himself.

Giancarlo had a lot to say about famous people he'd met, done business with, dated or married. There seemed to be quite a few on all fronts. Mrs. Entwhistle counted four ex-wives and marveled at the energy – and money - it must have taken to get in and out of all those relationships. Giancarlo was still talking.

Her thoughts strayed. Had she remembered to take out a carton of orange juice to thaw for tomorrow's breakfast? Maybe she and Max could stop at the bakery on the way home and get some of those good cinnamon rolls. Was the bakery open late?

"Now, remember, when the band starts playing, save the first dance for me," Giancarlo said, looking deep into Mrs. Entwhistle's eyes.

She couldn't think if she'd cleaned her trifocals before leaving home. These new non-reflective lenses attracted dirt and smears like twin magnets. Mrs. Entwhistle thought smugly that she hadn't needed cataract surgery yet. Had her mind always wandered like this, or did it only happen when she was bored?

Giancarlo cleared his throat importantly, signaling that he was about to say something significant. "I'm just wondering: do you ladies both own your own homes?"

"Why, yes, we do," Maxine answered. "We often say it's a shame we don't just share a place instead of maintaining two houses, but we're both attached to our homes and set in our ways, I guess."

"That's great, that's wonderful. And I bet both those houses are long paid for, am I right?"

They nodded, exchanging puzzled glances.

"Now here's what I want to talk to you about. Do you have any idea how much equity you're sitting on? Why, thousands and thousands of dollars! Did you know that you can get a reverse mortgage on your homes and free up a lot of extra spending money? Why should all that cash be tied up in your houses when you could use it to travel, or do some home repairs you've been putting off? Get a new car, maybe. And you'd never have to pay it back. How does that sound? Most of us could use some extra moolah, am I right?" Giancarlo smiled widely, his too-white teeth seeming to Mrs. Entwhistle like predatory fangs. "I can hook you up with a reputable finance company. You know me, you can trust me, and I'd be your agent, look out for your best interests and all that. What have you got to lose, am I right?"

"Well, your fee, for one thing. My house will be about all I have to leave my children," Mrs. Entwhistle said. "If I borrow against it, won't they have to pay it back when I'm gone?"

"Sure, sure, or let the house go back to the mortgage company. But what do you care? You won't be around to see it. We'll get you a bumper sticker for your new car that says, 'I'm spending my children's inheritance.' You don't owe your kids a dime, not a dime. Live it up while you're alive, that's what I always say. Am I right?"

"No, you're not right, and that's not what I always say," Mrs. Entwhistle said. She felt a flush of rage at Giancarlo for daring to slight her children, if only in theory. Her voice rose so that several people at nearby tables glanced at her. "I always say, don't take advantage of old friendships to try to sell something. That's what I always say."

Giancarlo's affable smile fled. "Well!" he said huffily, "I was just trying to help some old friends - senior citizens."

"We're all the same age," Maxine reminded him. "Same class, remember? And I don't want a reverse mortgage, either."

"Excuse me, ladies." Giancarlo rose with wounded dignity, crossed the room and approached another group. Maxine and Mrs. Entwhistle heard him say, "Good evening, good evening. How are you lovely ladies tonight? I'll bet every one of you comes from a beautiful home, am I right?"

"For heaven's sake," Mrs. Entwhistle said, shaking her head. "You just never know how people will turn out, do you?"

"Are you okay? Do you want to go home?" Maxine asked.

Mrs. Entwhistle suspected that Maxine knew about her secret crush, but she'd never, by hint, nudge or wink, reveal that she knew. Mrs.Entwhistle thought for the thousandth time that there couldn't be a better friend than Maxine.

"Go home? Not on your life," Mrs. Entwhistle said. "We haven't had dinner yet, and I'm hungry. Plus, I want to hear the class roll called so we can find out what happened to everybody and who-all is already dead."

"We know what happened to Giancarlo," Maxine said.

"We sure do. I just wonder how he got his teeth so white."

"Maybe by chewing up widows and orphans," Maxine suggested. They laughed in perfect harmony, as only old friends can laugh.

"I'm still glad I bought this dress, though," Mrs. Entwhistle said. "I might wear it again, who knows? It never hurts to look one's best. Am I right?"

Made in the USA
Monee, IL
29 August 2022